JUSTICE FOR THE SEAL

HERO FORCE BOOK FIVE

AMY GAMET

1

Logan O'Malley worked for a bunch of assholes.

He picked up his tequila and swirled it in a circle, staring into the liquid like it had the power to turn back time, to make him forget the things he'd heard that had knocked his world off its motherfucking axis.

Jax and Cowboy had killed a Navy SEAL. One of their own employees. An original member of HERO Force named Garrison Cole.

Allegedly.

He downed the rest of his drink in one gulp.

He could see now how stupid he was for looking up to them. How childish.

Naive.

Jax and Cowboy had sat him down in Cowboy's office, shutting the door even though the rest of the team was on a mission in Dubai. There was a lawsuit, Jax said. A civil case against the two of them for wrongful death.

But it was his face that fucked with Logan's brain.

Jax registered no emotion while he recounted the story of Cole's death. None at all. The leader of HERO Force was nothing if not pragmatic, but he could have been talking about a broken fax machine or running out of copy paper.

He was downright icy, and Logan had been filled with unease. No.

Suspicion.

The bartender poured him another drink.

Logan wasn't usually a guy to go with his gut. Analytics and proof, rational thought and logic. Science. But sitting in that room listening to Jax had his inner empath screaming.

They did it.

Jax and Cowboy fucking killed one of their own guys.

Logan probably wouldn't have found out about it at all, except now they needed his help.

Well, *they* didn't need it, exactly.

State Justice Anthony Royce did.

The crack of a cue ball was followed by the thud of balls dropping into pockets and Logan's eyes focused on the liquor bottles on the shelf in front of him. The bar smelled like cigarettes from a time when smoking had been allowed. It was stale and foul, just like his meeting an hour ago, the air conditioning barely cooling the humid air.

After the mind fuck of a meeting with Jax and Cowboy, they'd brought him into the conference room to meet Justice Royce. He looked so goddamn respectable sitting in the HERO Force conference room, he could have been on a commercial for a law firm.

That's when the dirty laundry really got pulled out from under the bed.

Jax and Cowboy explained Royce was the judge who'd dismissed the criminal charges against them, and now he was getting death threats.

That's when Logan started thinking of quitting his job.

His bosses were no better than the dirtbags HERO Force was always fighting back against.

You can go back to the NSA.

Hell, there were a hundred and one jobs he was qualified for. That wasn't the issue. The problem was he still wanted to work for the company he'd thought he was working for—where the men had integrity and fought for justice.

He hated himself in that moment. Hated the blind faith he'd allowed himself to have in these men. No wonder the other guys treated him like he was ten. He acted like a goddamn child.

Sure, he'd been working hard with Hawk, qualifying on weapons one by one, training in military strategy. But while he told himself it was just curiosity, the truth was he'd been trying to close the gap between him and the guys he looked up to. Especially Jax.

Jax, who was across the street at HERO Force headquarters with Justice Royce right now, probably getting their stories straight in case Royce was called to testify in the civil case. What a fucking joke.

You have a choice to make.

He could go to work on the Royce case like it was business as usual, or he could hand in his resignation. He took another sip of tequila.

I want out. Right. Fucking. Now.

No more HERO Force, no more Jax and no more trying to emulate people who weren't even worthy of his attention.

The street noise got louder and Logan turned to see Jax walk into the bar. He sat down next to Logan and ordered a whiskey. "You okay?" he asked.

"Now that I know you killed a man?"

"I told you how it happened."

"Yes, you did. Total accident. Could have happened to anybody."

"This isn't about me or Cowboy. This is about Royce. Someone related to the case wants him dead. That's where your attention needs to be focused, not on something that happened years before your time that doesn't affect you at all."

"Right. Royce. The man who behaves like a close personal friend of yours, but is actually the judge who dismissed murder charges against you and Cowboy."

"He wasn't a friend at the time."

"Because that would reek of impropriety on his part if he let his friends go free."

Jax set his drink on the bar with a thud. "I'm still co-commander of this team. You'd do well to remember that."

Logan knew he was pushing back too hard, but he couldn't seem to stop talking, stop picking at the scab that covered Jax's culpability.

He needed to see what was underneath, now that he knew his hero was made of flesh and blood. He had to know the depth of the darkness Jax had kept hidden from view. "I don't want to work for a man I don't respect."

Jax stared at him for a beat. "It was an accidental shooting."

Logan leaned in close. "Tell me what the fuck really happened, or I'm gone."

Jax seemed to focus far away, the silence stretching out to an uncomfortable void. When he finally spoke, his voice was low. "We had no choice." He met Logan's eyes. "We did it because we had no choice."

"Go on."

Jax shook his head. "All you need to know is none of this was Royce's fault. Now someone wants him dead, and it's our responsibility, Cowboy's and mine. If we could solve this without involving you, we'd do it. But you're the one with the skills we need, Logan. And you're just going to have to decide if you trust me."

"That's where you're wrong, Jax. You have to decide if you trust me."

An intense light flashed brightly through the window over Jax's shoulder, white light so bright it seemed to burn a hole in Logan's retinas.

"Get down!" yelled Logan, lowering his own head as he pulled down Jax. The sound erupted and the shock wave hit, shattering the window into the bar, spraying glass like water from a sprinkler.

Someone was screaming.

"Go, go, go!" barked Jax, but Logan was already on his feet, passing Jax as he pulled out his weapon. They ran into the blindingly sunny day, black smoke billowing from a sedan full of fire, fifteen-foot flames licking the sky.

A car bomb.

A figure could be seen in the car, barely human, covered in flames, and Logan rushed to the vehicle in an instinctual move to help the victim. The heat burst forth as if from the gates of hell but still he reached for the door, jerking back his hand when it was instantly burned.

He was ambushed from behind, Jax screaming in his ear as he pulled Logan away from the car, "Get back! You can't save them now." But Logan could still see the person on fire —dying right before his eyes.

"Jesus," yelled Jax. "The license plate! Look at the fucking license plate!"

Logan's eyes popped open, zeroing in on the piece of metal, a single word showing clear.

Justice.

"It's Royce," said Jax, his voice like a sob. "The motherfucker got Royce."

The smoke was noxious and Logan stumbled backward. He was inhaling the smell of gasoline and burning flesh, and he needed to vomit.

Sirens echoed in the distance.

There was nowhere to go, nothing to do but watch the car burn.

A firetruck arrived and firefighters hopped out, attacking the fire with long hoses until all that was left was a scorched black shell.

And what remained of a human being.

Logan had never been so close to death, seen it reach up from the depths of hell with gnarled fingers and rip someone from the earth. He thought of the man he'd just met upstairs and imagined his torched skeleton now covered in water.

He bent at the waist and threw up.

Cowboy boots appeared in his line of vision. "You need to find out who did this," said Cowboy. He sighed heavily. "I know you think what we did was wrong. I could see it in your eyes. But the judge didn't deserve to die like this."

Logan righted himself and looked at the other man. There was emotion in Cowboy's voice.

Regret.

"He was an innocent man who spent his life fighting for good over evil and someone burned him alive. I know your sense of justice is reeling right now." Cowboy pointed to the wreckage. "But that's where your anger should be directed. That's the greatest injustice of all. Help us catch the guys who did this, even if Jax and I aren't the heroes you thought we were."

It was a challenge. A request. A demand.

Jax crossed to them and narrowed his eyes at Logan, that steely stare that Logan had always found intimidating now seeming older, more pained. "Are you with us?" Jax asked.

They needed him. He was an integral part of this team, a vital gear in the machine that could find Justice Royce's killer.

And Logan knew he would continue to work for HERO Force. He would find out who was responsible for this and do everything in his power to bring them down.

He lifted his chin. "Yes."

"Good." Jax pointed out surveillance cameras. "I want video from those cameras, and I want it now."

2

Gemma Faraday parked and opened her car door, heat coming at her like she was opening a hot oven. She stood and started to sweat in the sunshine, her silk blouse still stuck to her back from the equally hot walk from the courthouse to her vehicle.

Day nine of record-high temperatures in Atlanta with no end in sight, and the weather was smothering her as surely as a well-placed pillow.

Her heels clicked on the pavement as she crossed to the nursing home, waves of heat from the asphalt making the building shimmy like a mirage. She thought of last night's news, death count from the heatwave now over a dozen, most of them elderly.

She walked through a revolving door and into the lobby, the icy air conditioning as welcome as the smell of old age was not. These elderly people weren't dead.

They just acted like it.

She smirked at a familiar nurse as she passed. "Hi, Laurie."

"He's waiting for you."

He doesn't even know who I am.

She grit her teeth to keep from stating the obvious and kept walking, telling herself the nurse was trying to be nice.

Click. Click. Click. Click.

Damn it. She was running late, her father's favorite news program long-since begun, her caseload weighing on her mind and waiting not-so-patiently for her to return to her chambers.

You don't need to come here anymore.

That nagging voice that longed to be free of this obligation was the devil on her shoulder. What was the point in visiting your father if he didn't even know who you were?

Because I know who he is, and I love him.

That was the point. She'd stand by her father's side for the rest of his life. It was important. Maybe the most important thing in her life.

The truth of the sentiment echoed in her mind. She was the only child of Al and Beverly Faraday, both only children themselves. Since her mother passed away, her father was the only family she had in the world.

There was no significant other, no husband or ex, the only real relationship of her life having ended years earlier —leaving her stronger, lonelier, and and more than a little bit sad.

She pushed into her father's room, struck as she always was by the complete lack of color in the space. There was beige in a multitude of hues, even a few specs of white, whereas in her memories, her father had always been surrounded by color.

It was a nice place. The best facility money could buy; her bank account could testify to that. Yet it was apropos that his room was a small square of space cut off from the rest of the world and operating completely independently from it.

She took in his sleeping form, so much smaller than it used to be. She touched his white hair and his eyes opened, confusion registering in their depths.

Her face fell. That look never got easier to take.

Last year, even, he'd recognized her as often as not. There were even days when they could talk about case law or her latest verdict—him debating the merits of the decision like the devil's advocate that he was.

You have a gift for the law, Gemma-girl.

She swallowed against the emotion in her throat and moved for the television, turning it on. "Time for the news. You like this." They were already doing the weather.

"We missed the beginning," he grumbled.

"You were sleeping."

"I was awake."

She pulled out her computer, half-listening to the television. More of the same. Hotter than hell with no relief in sight. Atlanta was always hot in summer, but this wasn't just hot, this was roasting—like chickens-in-a-grocery-store kind of roasting—and it made her cranky.

Her inbox had over a hundred unread messages. She sighed heavily while the news droned on in the background.

"It appears we made a mistake when we reported the car fire today in downtown Atlanta. Here again is the image we brought you at the top of the hour, an explosion we reported as having killed state justice Anthony Royce."

Gemma's head shot up. Video of firefighters putting out a car fire played on the screen. Everything in the room grew louder, as if her panic had amplified her hearing.

Royce who'd once said he loved her.

Royce who'd lied and broken her heart.

Royce who she stared down whenever their professional paths crossed, which was far too often.

The anchor cleared his throat. *"It appears that was a mistake. The occupant of the vehicle was in fact Barbara Royce, Anthony Royce's wife. She was pronounced dead at Grady Memorial Hospital."*

"Oh God, no," she whispered, holding her hand to her chest. The familiar guilt settled in her stomach like a stone. She'd once been responsible for hurting Royce's wife. Embarrassing her. Humiliating her. And now she was gone.

She'd seen Barbara at the Governor's Ball last fall, turning to catch the older woman staring at her from across the room. Their eyes met and held for several moments, a silent reckoning between them.

I'm so damn sorry.

Gemma imagined Barbara in that car, surrounded by flames. The terror she must have experienced. And the girls! They must be devastated.

"But in a bizarre twist, the FBI reports Justice Royce was abducted from the sidewalk near the explosion by two men as he approached the burning vehicle. The police department has released this video of the abduction, taken from a surveillance camera from a local business."

A grainy image of a sidewalk appeared as two men dressed in dark clothing hopped out of a light colored van. There on the right was a man with Royce's familiar gait and Gemma's mouth dropped open as she watched the other men grab him and throw him in the van.

"Wow," said the female newscaster.

"Wow indeed, Janet. Authorities are asking anyone with information about the crime to call Crimestoppers."

Royce had enemies, herself included. But what kind of motive could someone have for kidnapping?

Maybe he was dead, too.

She shut her laptop, her hands shaking. She needed to get out of here, get back to the office to see what people were saying. Maybe they knew something more than was being reported on the news.

How the hell had she missed the gossip this morning?

You were locked in your chambers, working.

She was always working, never socializing with the rest of the staff at the courthouse. It was safer to keep a coffeemaker in her chambers. Easier to keep bottled water than to face her coworkers.

"I have to go."

"It was nice to meet you," said her father.

"You too, Dad." She stood and walked briskly toward the door, calling over her shoulder, "See you tomorrow."

3

Gemma plopped onto the leather couch in her chambers feeling like a wet towel that had been wrung out. The car bombing and Royce's kidnapping had the courthouse turned on it's head even though he worked in a different building—with heightened security and the gossip mill buzzing to a nearly audible hum.

She hadn't learned anything new about the incident, and she certainly hadn't expected the majority of the gossip to be about her.

It was like the past eight years hadn't happened, and she was right back there, Anthony Royce's mistress who'd slept her way to the top.

A knock on the door to her chambers and she squeezed her eyes shut. "Come in."

A woman with short black hair pushed into the room, her best friend, April. They'd been roommates in college and had remained close ever since. "I got out of work as early as I could, sweetie."

"Did we have plans?" asked Gemma, racking her brain.

"No, I just figured you'd appreciate a friendly face. I think you need a drink."

"I don't want a drink."

"Your ex-lover's been kidnapped and his wife's been killed by a bomb. Honey, if anyone needs a drink, you do."

Gemma shivered at the thought of Barbara Royce's fiery death. "She didn't deserve to die like that. She didn't deserve any of it."

"This has nothing to do with you and Royce. Don't go there."

"How can I not?"

"Because you didn't know he was married! You're not a psychic, for God's sake. He lied to you. It's been eight years. Stop blaming yourself."

"Do you think she stopped blaming me?"

"We're going out for drinks. Now."

"No."

"I'm not asking, I'm telling."

"I have work to do, even if I'm not in court."

"And you're really able to get it done today? Like this? You look like shit. Clearly your mind is other places, so take it home with you if you need to, but get the hell out of this office and away from the people who are looking at you sideways."

Not again.

Gemma's shoulders dropped. "You noticed that, too."

"Hell yes. Your secretary was tripping over her tongue talking about you. Get your purse."

She swiped at her eyes, unaware she'd been crying. She didn't feel like going out. She felt like going home and sobbing in a quiet, dark room. "I know you're trying to help, but I just want to go home."

"I know you. You're going to beat yourself up until your

soul is black and blue, then you're going to stay up all night worrying about Royce."

"Which is exactly what I should be doing right now."

April took her by the elbow. "Well, too bad, because you're coming with me."

Gemma let herself be dragged from her chambers, past her secretary who yes—*damn it*—had an all-knowing look on her face. The rumors had nearly derailed Gemma's career eight years earlier, rumors that were mostly true.

The only part that was pure fiction was the notion that the affair had gotten her the judicial nomination. That wasn't true at all.

But it sure as hell looked true.

She'd been a hair's breadth away from moving to a new town and starting over when things started to improve, then one day the rumors were gone.

Well, now they're making a comeback.

She sighed heavily, even as she knew she was grateful for her friend's pushy intervention. "Okay. We'll go out. But I don't want to go to a dance club."

"Fine. We'll go to that bar you like on Peachtree."

4

Logan walked down the crowded street, lights from restaurants and bars shining in the haze. Nighttime seemed just as hot as the day, the air clammy and still. He was aware of the people around him, but all he could see was the burning car and the one woman he couldn't save.

Royce's wife.

Logan wanted to find the guy who did this and make him pay. He wanted to strap him into a car and make him burn alive like he'd done to that poor woman.

He squeezed his hand with the bandaged palm, pain screaming along his nerve endings. He wasn't ready to go home, couldn't imagine falling asleep, and he'd found himself back in front of HERO Force headquarters where the explosion had taken place.

He'd walked in one big fucking circle.

Of course you did. Where the hell else are you going to go?

Two women stood on the sidewalk with their backs to him, and he stopped walking, listening to their conversation. One of them was crying. The other put her arm around her and said, "They'll find him. Royce is a badass. He's going to be okay."

Adrenaline shot into his bloodstream. Gone was the lost soul who'd been searching for meaning in the middle of destruction. He was back on the job in a heartbeat.

He narrowed his eyes. Who were these two? Coworkers of Royce? Maybe friends?

"The pavement," said one. "Look at the pavement."

The other woman nodded. "I know, it's fucking terrible."

Logan's eyes went to the blackened asphalt and he remembered the acrid smell of the flames that had caused it.

"Let's get you home," said the other.

"I don't want to go home. I don't think I could stand it."

"Then come with me to the club."

"Fine. I don't care anymore."

Logan followed them, his mind working to put the pieces together. Was this woman having an affair with Royce?

He wanted to see her face. Get a name. She didn't seem to know where Royce was, but surely she was involved with him somehow.

The women walked several blocks until the *thump-thump-thump* of music could be heard floating on the air, then he followed them into a dance club, throngs of people pressed together and moving.

He let himself get caught in the flow of humanity away from the women, wanting to get some space between them and himself so he wouldn't appear too conspicuous.

The music was loud, bass rumbling through his body. He scanned the crowd, his eyes catching on exposed flesh and short skirts, men groping women on the dance floor. The entire space stood in sharp contrast to the rest of his day like sunshine against the darkest night, and his cock suddenly ached with need.

Fuck.

Exactly.

The scientist in him knew what was happening. Sex was the antidote for death, the epitome of living, and he craved it in that moment like a drowning man desperate for land beneath his feet.

He forced the feelings down. He had to find out who the women were, had to do something to fight the atrocities of the day that were scarred into his brain. He needed to stay focused, no matter how much he wanted a woman who knew how to fuck and could make it okay until the sun came up tomorrow.

He had to find out who those women were, what their connection was to Royce. At least get a good look at them, if not their names. His eyes found them at the other end of the bar.

Now that he could see their faces, his interest piqued, his inappropriate lust crashing into his professional responsibility. The shorter one was stunning. A little older, just like he liked. She looked like a big-chested librarian in a tight skirt, just begging for someone to rip it off her.

His cock tingled.

No. Fucking. Way.

It was a terrible idea to pursue her.

Or was it? They were in a club filled with people looking to hook up. He wanted information and he wanted sex. Even as he silently gave himself permission, he knew it was a bad idea.

A terrible idea he could barely wait to act on.

5

It was dark, with bursts of light rhythmically flashing here and there. Gemma closed her eyes. She was drunk.

More drunk than was wise.

Normally, she was good for splitting a bottle of wine over dinner, but this was out of hand. She'd gone in search of numbness and had found sweet oblivion.

Her eyes shot across the dance floor to where April gyrated against a man with light brown skin and short curly hair. She wondered if her friend would take him home.

I wish I could do that.

The thought surprised her. After the stress of this day, Royce's disappearance and the brush of death on the edges of her life, she desperately needed human contact.

She wanted to make love.

That's when she noticed a man looking at her. A young guy, maybe thirty, with a body like a department store mannequin. She resisted the urge to look behind her for the younger, more attractive girl he was gawking at.

Let it be me.

Her eyes wandered over that beautiful body of his. The men she dated were long past that strong and sexy stud phase. Sure, most of them were fit, taking good care of themselves and aging as well as they could, but you just didn't find a forty-five-year-old guy who looked like that man did over there.

Not even close.

Did the women he dated know how good they had it? With his ready erection and what she was sure must be his endless energy? Hell, she couldn't even remember the last time she dated a man who didn't have at least some gray hair. If he had any hair at all.

Time was hard on men.

Hard on.

She laughed to herself and the man cocked his head, his stare questioning. She raised her glass to him.

If you only knew what I was thinking right now.

He headed Gemma's way.

Fuck.

He was incredibly tall and walked like a big cat, all sway and muscle. When he reached her he bent down and said in her ear, "What's so funny?"

He smelled like the quintessential male, as if nature had created him to lure her like a flower lured the bees. "Honestly? You don't want to know."

"That makes me want to know even more. Would you like to dance?"

"No." She held her hands up to ward him off. "I mean, I'd like to, but I'm not a dancer."

"Then just hang on to me." He took her hand and pulled her onto the dance floor, never breaking their stare. She liked the feel of his long, strong fingers wrapped around hers. Was it true what they said about the size of a man's hands and the size of his penis? She giggled again. So damn drunk.

There was a bandage on his hand. "What happened?" she asked.

"Just a burn."

He took her in his arms, swaying to the beat. She copied him. "Relax," he said, his voice smoky and deep.

Why the hell not? Her eyes were stuck on his chest, and she longed to feel it with her hands. Her insides were melting like candle wax next to a flame. What would those sculpted muscles feel like under her eager fingers?

Stop it, Gemma.

She shouldn't be thinking about this guy like that. Not when it was making her heart race and her back arch, so that her breasts jutted forward against his body.

"You're very beautiful," he said.

She opened her mouth to shrug off the compliment but his stare dropped to her lips and she froze. There was so much sex in that one single look—more sex than she'd had in her bed for the last few years, easily—and she wanted it.

She wanted all of it.

She lifted her chin and met his mouth in a scorching kiss. He tasted like mint and he smelled like spicy leather, an intoxicating fragrance she wanted to inhale and keep forever inside her.

Still the music played, the pounding beat resonating between her legs, seemingly in sync with the steady pulse that hammered there. The room fell away, leaving just the two of them and her body's overwhelming response to this man.

His hands were around her waist, pulling her tightly against him, and his hard body felt every bit as good as she'd hoped it would.

She should stop. Shouldn't she? The petulant child inside her rebelled. Other people got to do these things, have these experiences. Hell, April did it all the time. How come she never could? The answer to her unspoken question rose up in her mind, the same answer she'd relied on to get her life back on track after the affair.

Walk the straight and narrow.

Don't do anything reprehensible.

No casual sex.

Expect everything to come out in the open, and when it does, know that you will be able to hold your head high.

His mouth moved to her neck, and her head fell back with the glorious sensation. Maybe just this once she could live her life without her past dictating what she should do. Maybe just for this night she could be someone who wasn't so goddamn careful.

She needed to be touched, desperately.

One hand snaked up her back while the other moved lower, cupping her bottom and pulling her firmly against his erection. When she would have moved back, he whispered in her ear.

"Do you see what you're doing to me?"

She knew it was a line. Probably one he'd used a hundred times, but she didn't care. She wanted to be that person. Wanted to be capable of driving a guy like this crazy with desire.

You're drunk, Gemma.

Go home.

Yes, that's what she needed to do. Quickly, before she could change her mind.

She pushed away from him, surprised when the movement made her head swim. She needed to find April. She would pull her back from this cliff she wanted to jump off.

That's what friends were for. "I need to go to the ladies' room."

He nodded and yelled over the music, "I'll wait here."

Spinning around, her eyes raked over the crowd. Was it darker in here than it had been before? Everything seemed more intense, overwhelming. She pushed through people, her body seeming to brush intimate parts of everyone as she made her way off the dance floor. She hated this shit, hated dance clubs.

Why the hell did I let April bring me here?

She caught sight of her friend up ahead, and pulled her away from the man she was dancing with, into the ladies' room.

"What's wrong?" asked April.

"I want to go home."

"Really?" She laughed. "Because you looked like you're having one hell of a time with that guy."

"Yeah. Ten more minutes of making out and my clothes would be all over the floor."

"Would that be so bad?"

"I don't even know him."

"Some of the best sex of my life was with guys I didn't know."

Gemma rolled her eyes. "You know I can't do this shit."

April dug in her purse and withdrew a condom. "*Au contraire.* You can do this shit, and I think you should."

Gemma took the condom from her friend's hand, looking at it questioningly. "I have a condom in my purse."

"It's probably been there since college. Use mine."

"Today of all days, you don't see why this is a bad idea?"

"Today of all days is the reason you should do it. You've been beating yourself up about Royce for eight years. Eight fucking years, Gemma! Let it go already. You made a mistake. We all make them. But you've been living in some sort of prison you made for yourself, and the only time you come out – really come out – is for some public flagellation."

Gemma could feel her cheeks heating. "That's not true."

"It is true." April opened the bathroom door, the music and that tribal beat now filling the ladies' room. "You need to go and get laid."

Gemma turned and looked at herself in the mirror. Her hair was falling out of its tame style, auburn curls framing her face. The little makeup she had put on for work had virtually disappeared, save for a light touch of mascara that framed her hazel eyes.

She was ordinary.

Her eyes caught on the little lines fanning out from the corners of her eyes.

And I'm getting old as fuck.

Old as fuck and alone. And responsible – oh so responsible! And what did she have to show for it? Really show for it? Her career, of course. Everything had been about her career for so long, she could almost make herself forget she had ever wanted anything more.

But she had.

A quiet voice deep inside her remembered. She had wanted things she knew now would never be a part of her life. She thought she'd made her peace with that.

She was okay with it.

Except suddenly she wasn't okay with anything. She wasn't okay with her tied-up hair, or her white blouse and navy skirt, or the lack of excitement she'd guaranteed with her walk on the straight and narrow.

She reached up and pulled at the bobby pins that held her hairstyle in place, as if each one represented a decision that had gotten her to this place where she was so afraid of everything, including that guy out there who had probably moved on to somebody else by now.

She tucked the condom into her purse and stepped back into the dance club. She pushed past people, no longer concerned when her body brushed theirs. She was part of it now, part of this room and the energy here, but her mind was on the man she left on the dance floor.

If he really was waiting for her, she would go to him. And whatever would be, would be.

6

It took a serious amount of willpower for Logan to keep his hands on top of Gemma's clothes during the cab ride back to his apartment. He wanted to explore her skin with a desperate kind of lust he'd rarely experienced. He explored every inch of her body as she stroked the hard ridge of his erection through his jeans.

He hadn't expected her to come back, but she had—her hair down and free and curling around her shoulders like a fucking prom queen.

He'd thought she was beautiful the first time he'd seen her, but it had been an untouchable sort of beauty, polished and clean and so far out of his league he almost took himself out of the lineup before he even got up to bat. But when she came back to him, she was beautiful like a pinup. A movie star. A sex goddess. And her eyes told him clearly that was exactly what she wanted to be.

Who is this woman to Royce?

He shouldn't be taking her home without the answer to that question, but he didn't care half as much as he should. On the contrary, the fact that she had some association with the jarring events of his day seemed predestined. She was meant to be the one he would fuck tonight.

His hand fisted in the fabric of her blouse, tugging it free from her skirt and touching the soft skin beneath. Already he had mapped out her body with his fingers and palms, knew the fullness of her breasts and the curve of her hips that awaited him.

She moaned against his mouth as the car made a sharp turn, pressing her more tightly against his body. His eyes flashed to the window, the familiar streetlights telling him they were only blocks away.

Thank God.

He couldn't take much more of this woman driving him crazy.

He'd had a hard-on for nearly two hours and they needed some privacy before he stripped this woman bare and fucked her in the back of a taxi.

They pulled up to the curb and he hastily paid the driver, knowing he was tipping too much but refusing to wait for change. He pulled Gemma behind him into the building, yanked open the elevator gate and nearly pushed her inside.

She was ready for him. Of course she was. She was with him every step of the way, meeting every touch with a more intense one of her own, welcoming his kisses and raising him, every time.

He pressed her against the wall of the elevator, hiking up her skirt, grabbing onto the soft flesh of her ass and kneading it with his hands. She lifted a leg, wrapping it around his hip, and he thrust against the fabric of her underwear.

The elevator ground to a halt and he threw open the gate, quickly unlocking the door to his apartment and dragging her inside like a caveman pulling her into his cave. That was what it felt like, this all-consuming need to possess her. And if the noises she was making were any indication, she liked it when he was rough with her.

He slammed the door behind them, long shadows covering the floor with ribbons of light and darkness. It was empty in here, more space than he had furniture, and their heavy breathing seemed to echo against the floor and walls.

She pulled at his shirt, sending buttons scattering, and he yanked her blouse over her head, tossing it away. She reached for his belt buckle.

"We need a bed," he said.

"No. I want you right here." She unbuckled his belt and unbuttoned the fly of his jeans. His cock sprang free and she moved lower, taking him in her hot, wet mouth.

Jesus.

She took him deep and his balls clenched tightly. He threaded his fingers through her hair and held her to him.

She came up for air. "You're so big."

Fuck, he couldn't take this anymore. He had to be inside her. He scooped her up and headed for the bedroom.

She kissed the side of his neck. "Where are we going?"

He chuckled. "The floor is concrete. It's cold. But it looks cool, and the chicks dig it." He threw her on the bed.

She stared up at him in her skirt and bra, legs slightly spread as she propped herself up on her elbows, making her tits thrust forward. "You bring a lot of girls here?"

He climbed between her legs and squeezed her breasts in the darkness. "Some." He licked along the edge of her bra, savoring the taste of her skin. "Is that a problem for you?"

"No. That's what I want."

"What do you mean?"

"Just sex. I want sex that doesn't mean anything."

He ran his hand along her thigh, pushing up her skirt, then moved lower and settled his face between her legs. "Do you want it to be good?"

"Yes."

He pulled her panties down her legs and tossed them to the floor. He kissed the inside of her thigh, noting how she jumped before relaxing into the sensation. He traced the folds of her sex gently with his finger. "Really good?"

She whispered huskily. "Yes."

He found her entrance wet and slick, and traced her sensitive opening before slipping his finger inside her heat. She bucked against him and he bent his head, gently licking her sensitive bud. "But you don't want it to mean anything."

"No."

"You want me to fuck you and make you come until you can barely lift your head off the pillow."

She was panting now. "Oh, yes." She unzipped her purse and handed him a condom.

Her voice was begging him, daring him, beseeching him. He sheathed himself with one practiced motion and settled himself between her legs, pushing himself inside her. With one fierce thrust he buried himself completely. She let out a loud gasp and he forced himself to be still, sure he'd hurt her.

Her hands skated over his back and down lower, pulling his hips against her while her body squeezed him tightly. "God, you feel so good," she said.

He pumped into her, retreating and thrusting again. He didn't even know this woman, didn't know her name, but his body knew hers in an instant. It was as if he recognized her, and he wondered if she'd let Royce fuck her like this.

She moaned loudly, her body tightening around him as

she found her release. Still he fought his need to climax until she clutched at him in relief, his body launching into a powerful orgasm that left him shaking.

He rolled onto his back, taking her with him. He kissed the top of her head.

"I'm Logan."

He felt her smile against his chest. "Gemma."

An uncommon name. That would help him find her. She wanted no-strings-attached sex, but she was somehow involved in his case, and he already knew there was no way in hell one night with her in his bed was going to be enough.

They had chemistry, and he wanted to fuck her until that spark petered out. His cock bounced with renewed interest. "Hope you don't have to get up too early tomorrow," he said.

"Ugh. I do."

"What do you do?"

"I'm a lawyer. You?"

That was probably how she knew Royce, but it still didn't tell them much about their relationship. And now she wanted to know where he worked. He hesitated.

How close was Gemma to Royce?

Close enough for him to confide in her about his meeting with HERO Force?

He noted her loose, relaxed limbs, the way she cuddled easily in his arms, and paid careful attention when he spoke. "I work for a company called HERO Force. Hands-on Engagement and Recognizance Operations. We help people in trouble and keep them safe."

Her body registered no recognition.

"For a fee," she said with an easy laugh.

He flipped over quickly, rolling on top of her. "Hell yes.

Chick magnet apartments like this don't come cheap." He kissed her mouth, loving the taste of her and the way her legs spread willingly beneath him. "I hope you don't have any important lawsuits to file tomorrow, because I don't think you're going to get a lot of sleep." He pressed his hard cock against her.

"Oh my God, you're like a machine."

"I'll take that as a compliment." He took a condom out of the nightstand, put it on, and eased inside her. He groaned at the sensation. "I needed this today, Gemma. I needed you."

"Me, too."

This time when they moved together, it felt to Logan like their minds were connected as well as their bodies. She held his head in her hands and kissed him tenderly.

It was intense.

Too intense.

He pulled back. "Get on all fours."

She did as he asked and he thrust into her fully, letting his eyes close. He pumped hard into her body, loving the way she responded to him. He grabbed a handful of her hair, pulling her head back, and her body clenched tightly around his cock.

She liked that, too. *How rough would she let him get?*

He couldn't escape their connection, and he finally let himself go, feeling the click of one soul against another as they fit solidly into place, awareness focusing to a single point of pleasure.

7

"Earth to O'Malley."

Logan looked away from his site picture on the AK-47 to eyeball Trevor. "I'm listening."

"Then what the fuck did I just say?"

Trevor returned from Dubai ahead of the others, just in time for their weekly target practice at the outdoor range.

"That I have to take the wind speed and distance to target into consideration, not just the site picture." He knew he was distracted. Hell, anybody could tell he was distracted, and the hickey on his neck was only part of the reason why. The image of the car bomb was still lodged firmly in his mind, blocking the way for rational thought and conversation.

Not to mention Gemma had gotten away this morning without him knowing her relationship to Anthony Royce.

"Okay then, fire when ready."

Logan looked back down the barrel of the gun to his target some hundred yards away and pulled the trigger, emptying his magazine.

"Bring it back," said Hawk.

Logan hopped to his feet and reeled in the target.

Hawk spit on the ground. "I'm guessing whatever is on your mind has a kick ass pair of tatas and a cooch that just won't quit."

Logan grinned. Easier to talk about sex than death, any day. "That, she does."

"If you are in the field, shit like that will get you killed." The paper target came into view, a hole the size of an egg blown through the heart. Hawk whistled. "Nice grouping."

"If this is me getting killed, maybe I ought to think about those kick ass tatas and cooch more often."

Hawk met his eyes. "Do it again, smart ass. Two hundred yards this time."

Logan nodded and sent another target down the outdoor range.

"We rely on each other in the field, Logan. We need the complete attention of the entire team. Frankly I don't give a shit if you're good at multitasking. I want your whole brain with me when the bullets are flying."

Logan nodded. Hawk was testing him. The other guys were always testing him, and Logan appreciated it. Not everybody who wanted to learn this shit got trained by some of the best in the world. And if that meant he had to take some of their crap, then so be it.

"So, tell me about this girl," said Hawk.

"Woman."

Hawk chuckled. "I've seen you at the bars. The girls love that brainy geek thing you've got going on. So why do you pick the cougars?"

"Don't make it sound like they're hunting for prey. I picked her because I wanted her."

"What's the attraction?"

"A girl doesn't know what she wants. A woman does."

"You mean sex?"

It was Logan's turn to laugh. "I mean everything."

"And this woman wanted you?"

An image of Gemma riding him in the night popped into his mind. "Oh yeah, she did."

"How long you been seeing her?"

"Just one night. But I'm going to see her again, don't you worry."

Hawk shook his head. "If I didn't have the most beautiful Academy Award nominee in my bed every night, I might be a little jealous of you, boy."

"You won the freaking lottery with that one. When are you going to make an honest woman out of her?"

"Just as soon as she lets me. She wants to get through shooting one more movie first so she'll have time to plan everything. She'll be on location in Paris for six months."

"Damn, that's rough."

"Nothing we can't handle if we're going to make it 'till death do us part. Now fire that gun."

Logan got in prone position and lined up his sight, mentally calculating the effect of the wind on his projectile. He imagined the black outline was an actual tango, knowing it would feel different to fire at a real person.

His role with HERO Force was changing into something more tactical. The more he learned about combat and martial arts, the more was expected of him from the team. But his medical degree had taught him how to repair the damage from a bullet wound, not to inflict one, and he was quickly learning that supporting a righteous cause from a distance was very different than defending it himself.

He emptied his magazine and hopped back up, reeling it in. "You remember the first time you fired with the the intent to kill?"

"Of course I do. Everybody does."

"Tell me about it."

"It's a lot like losing your virginity. My story won't be anything like yours. When you're in the moment, you'll know what you need to do. The trick is actually doing it."

8

Gemma had barely slept. She was awake with the first light of dawn streaming through Logan's huge loft windows, her head throbbing as images of the night before ran through her mind.

Logan had given her everything she'd wanted in spades. Physical gratification and the most basic connection with another human being.

Now she needed to go back to real life.

Her worry for Royce was waiting at the edges of her memory since she'd refused to stew on it last night.

It had been years since she and Royce were together, but she'd cared for him deeply before she learned of his duplicity. She'd done the right thing and ended their relationship when she found out he was married, but her heart was already broken. Hatred had quickly filled in those cracks.

Now he was in danger and she was filled with anxious worry, not only for Royce but for his family.

They must be going through hell.

Again.

She'd been responsible for putting them through it once

before. Now the girls' mother was dead and their father abducted. They must be grown up by now, but surely that didn't make it any easier.

Logan stirred behind her and she held her breath. Now that sobriety had taken hold, she couldn't believe she'd spent the night with a guy half her age, and all she wanted to do was escape.

She managed to slip from his bed and out of the apartment without waking him, then stopped home for a quick shower before heading to work.

Two hours later, she was staring into space, barely paying attention as she filled her mug with hot water and picked up a tea bag before settling behind her desk. She had a full schedule today, and she struggled to focus her attention on the matters at hand.

She flipped through correspondence and motions, upcoming cases and influential verdicts. She was just about to put her paperwork aside when her eyes locked onto a familiar name.

HERO Force.

Her head jerked back, not understanding why her one-night-stand's employer was staring her in the face. She skimmed the paperwork on the latest case she'd been assigned.

Stewart Cole versus Jax Andersson and Leo Wilson. An amount of money that made her whistle and an allegation of wrongful death.

She cursed colorfully.

I have a real knack for sleeping with the wrong guy.

She'd have to recuse herself. Her eyes squeezed shut. It happened. It was a small world with only six degrees of separation that sometimes felt like two or three.

She would handle it.

You're just feeling like a slut for sleeping with that guy last night. That's the problem.

An image of him on top of her appeared unbidden in her mind. She shook her head. Sorry wasn't the word. Her thighs were sore from straddling his large frame and there was a tenderness deep inside her from the repeated thrusts of his body into hers. The sex had been amazing, but she wasn't the type for one-night stands, and she liked him more than she probably should, especially since he was clearly much younger than she.

The clock chimed. It was time for voir dire in her first case, and she took a deep, cleansing breath before donning her robe and making her way into the courtroom.

As a judge in civil court, she'd seen everything from wrongful death like the HERO Force case to slander and breach of contract. Some of the cases were heartbreaking, but the one today was personal and she'd been dreading it for weeks.

It was a medical malpractice case being brought by the mother of a young woman who had died of breast cancer the year before. The patient was the same age Gemma had been when she was diagnosed with breast cancer herself.

Gemma had lived.

This woman's daughter had died.

It was hard to make sense of that, no matter the details of the case, and she wouldn't hear those for quite some time. It was her job to be impartial, but she was only human. Some cases affected her more than others, and she needed to work hard to keep her emotions in check and her judgment free from bias.

Jury selection could be a long process in a case like this, and two hours later they'd barely made any progress. The head lawyer for the doctor's team stood up. "Your honor, we request numbers three, five, and nine be excused."

She nodded. Those people had close relationships with people who'd had breast cancer. The damn disease was everywhere. If they hoped to avoid jurors who hadn't been touched by it in some way, they had a long road ahead of them.

She crossed her arms over her chest, thinking of a T-shirt she had in her closet at home that she should wear under her robe sometime during this trial.

Yes, they're fake.

My real ones tried to kill me!

Oh God, had Logan noticed?

Don't think about him again.

But her mind went rogue and her cheeks flooded with heat as she wondered what he might have noticed about her chest. She'd only had one other relationship since her surgery – a six month stint with a cardiologist – and he knew about her reconstruction long before they'd had sex. But Logan had no idea, and it had been very dark in the room and she'd kept her bra on.

Stop it.

She tapped her pencil on her blotter, wishing the lawyers would *do something* so she could get the hell out of her own head.

There was something about Logan that wasn't going to be easy to forget, and she hadn't bargained on that in her quest for anonymous sex. There had been moments during the night when it felt like they'd been lovers for years.

A kiss.

A touch.

His fingers intertwined with hers.

And his body! He was hung. She'd never been with a

guy like that, had barely believed April when she told her men of such size existed, like unicorns or Sasquatch. And the man had stamina. They'd had sex four times in the night, the intimacy of being woken from sleep by sexy kisses and erotic touches still at the forefront of her mind.

Definitely not easy to forget.

The lawyer moved forward to question a potential juror and she snapped back to the present, but it wasn't long before voir dire turned to quiet consideration and her mind was right back in Logan's bed.

Man, how old is he, anyway?

That might be a question she really didn't need answered. He looked about thirty. If that estimate was right, she was a solid fifteen years older than him. Hell, if this were *Teen Mom* she could be his mother.

She still had that thought in her mind several hours later after she'd adjourned the case for the night and finished some work in her chambers before heading home, exhausted.

It was dusk by the time she got off the bus near her house and started the three-block walk to her door. The evening air was warm and humid, a breeze carrying the smell of barbecue and flowers. For the first time all day, her mind was finally free of the buzzards that had been haunting her consciousness since she awoke.

A noise behind her and she turned, relieved to see it was just a jogger. Her neighborhood was pretty safe, but she was always conscious of the inherent dangers of a woman walking alone at night.

She moved to the side as he approached, when suddenly she was knocked hard to the ground, the man on top of her and the foul stink of body odor all around.

"What are you doing?" she exclaimed. She twisted her

head in an attempt to see him, but only caught part of a plastic mask.

Oh my God.

The man's voice was a harsh whisper in her ear. "You listen to me, Judge Faraday. If you ever want to see Anthony Royce alive again, you will do exactly what I tell you."

9

Logan walked into the HERO Force conference room, the sun shining brightly outside the wide windows. He'd already searched the Internet for information on Gemma while he had his morning coffee, coming up with one vital piece she'd left out herself.

She wasn't just a lawyer. She was a judge, just like Royce, though she worked in civil court, not criminal.

Noah and Austin were sitting with Cowboy and Hawk. "How was Dubai?" asked Logan.

"Kicked some ass. Took some names. The usual," said Austin. "Noah took a bullet in the ass."

"Grazed my ass, dickhead. A bullet grazed my ass."

"That's gonna leave a scar," said Austin.

Jax walked in, slamming the door behind him. Logan couldn't help but notice he looked like shit. "As you know, Justice Royce was kidnapped yesterday. I am making it our mission to personally locate him and assure his safety. The FBI is working the case, but I don't trust them to get the job done as well as my own men."

Logan tapped his pen. "Maybe we can get them to cooperate with us, share information—"

Jax nodded curtly. "That would be nice. It would also be nice if I would sprout wings and shoot rainbows out of my ass, but that isn't going to happen, either. Treat this like any other assignment. We bust our asses through any means necessary to find these motherfuckers and take them down."

"Hawk," said Cowboy. "You and Austin go to Royce's house and do a complete search. Any documents, anything. Interview his children. See what you can find out about motive."

Hawk's arms crossed against his chest like a bouncer. "The FBI won't appreciate the company."

"Royce's daughters are expecting you and will allow you into the house. If the feds don't like it, amuse them with stories about your famous girlfriend."

"Done."

Cowboy turned to Noah. "You're going with Jax and me to check on Stewart Cole, the plaintiff in the civil suit against us."

"Civil suit?" asked Noah.

"Try to keep your ass out of the line of fire this time," said Jax, ignoring Noah. He withdrew a computer from a leather bag and pushed it toward Logan. "This is Royce's laptop. I want to know everything he knew. Find out who's sending the threatening emails and anything else that might have been going on. It's a knee-jerk reaction to think this is related to the HERO Force case and it might be, but it might be something else entirely."

"What HERO Force case?" asked Noah.

"The one where Cowboy and I are being accused of murdering a member of HERO Force."

Noah's eyes got wide.

"Good. Glad we cleared that up," said Jax.

Austin chuckled. "See that? Your ass was in the way again."

Logan opened the computer. "Do you have a password for me?"

Jax handed him a sticky note. Logan typed it in and went to the email application. He whistled. "There are more than thirty thousand emails here."

"All read, I hope."

"Yeah, but not by me." He closed the computer. "It's going to take some time. Can I bring this home?"

Jax nodded. "We're counting on you, Doc. We can't get access to his court documents. We can't get into his office. We've got nothing to go on but that laptop and whatever we find at his house."

Seven hours later, Logan had organized the emails into folders using keywords, which eliminated a lot of the detritus. He was left with six thousand two hundred messages that needed to be read when he finally packed up his things and headed home for the night.

Home.

The last time he was in his apartment, Gemma was with him, naked in his bed.

Hell, lots of women had been in his bed, but the memory of that one grabbed him by the balls. She was a jumble of contradictions. Tame and wild. Sexually greedy with a shade of innocence that made him want to corrupt her. Anonymous and much too familiar all at the same time.

He thought of the way she'd emerged from the bathroom at the club, her hair down, oozing sex appeal where she'd been the untouchable professional just moments before. Of course he'd touched her anyway.

He'd do anything to keep touching her.

It figured he'd been drawn to a woman who only wanted sex. Yet another juxtaposition. He was used to being the one who only wanted to get off, constantly keeping a relationship at bay. Now she'd captivated his interest and she wanted nothing to do with him in the light of day.

She'd been long gone when he woke up this morning.

He stepped outside. It was hot and raining hard, thunder rumbling in the distance, and he jogged to his car. The laptop was shielded from the rain by a leather bag, but he wasn't so lucky. In the fifty feet from the building to his car, he'd gotten completely soaked.

The Ferrari's powerful engine roared to life. The car was his baby. Cowboy had once called it Logan's girlfriend, joking that it was the only curvy thing that would let him touch it.

If he only knew how wrong he was.

In his mind, he could see his hand grazing Gemma's naked hip. He clenched the wheel tighter, his hands aching to stroke her again, and he cursed under his breath. A flash of lightning illuminated the empty street.

It was late, he was tired and he would have liked the company of a woman. One woman in particular.

Gemma Faraday.

He parked in the lot across from his apartment and took off through the rain once more. He almost didn't notice her in the shadows, just to the side of the entrance to his building.

"Logan?"

Recognition was instantaneous and his dick leaped in his pants. She'd come back for an encore performance, as if he'd conjured her with his thoughts. He moved close to her, already anticipating their kiss, when he realized she was crying.

He cupped her face in his hands. She had an abrasion from below her cheekbone to high on her temple. "What happened?"

"I'm sorry to just show up here like this. I didn't know where else to go."

"It's okay." He steered her into the building, opening the door with a wave of his keychain.

"You said you help people."

He tilted his head. "Yeah. What's going on?"

Her lip trembled for a moment before her face crumpled. "I really need help."

10

Gemma looked small to Logan, curled up on the couch beneath the blanket his grandmother had knitted for him. He'd cleaned her abrasion and treated it with some ointment, her hair was wet, and her hands were wrapped around a cup of hot tea.

The muscles of his arms twitched. "Did he hurt you?"

"Besides my face? No."

Logan exhaled the breath he'd been holding. "Did you see what he looked like?"

"No. He was wearing a mask."

He could tell she'd been traumatized, but so far she was holding her own.

"He knew my name," she said. Her hands started to shake and she put down the tea. "He was talking in my ear, his voice all weird and echo-y from the mask, and he said if I wanted to see Royce alive again, I had to do what he told me to do."

Logan was careful to keep his face expressionless. "Royce?"

"He's a judge. A state justice, actually." She covered her eyes with the heels of her hands. "He was kidnapped yesterday, and his wife was killed. Did you see it on the news?"

"The car bomb."

"Yes. That's why my friend dragged me out for drinks."

"You were upset."

She nodded. "Very."

"Was he a friend of yours?"

"A long time ago. Not anymore."

"Boyfriend?"

She hesitated. "No."

"Then why would the kidnapper come to you? Did he ask for ransom?"

"Not exactly." She covered her face. "He wanted me to do something. I can't tell you what."

"You came to me because you wanted help. I can't help if you don't tell me the whole story."

"They're going to kill Royce if they find out I told anyone."

Not if we find him first.

He couldn't tell her HERO Force was looking for Royce, couldn't tell her he knew any more about the case than he already had.

Not yet, anyway.

Their worlds were overlapping, two circles that shared more common ground than he realized when he took her to his bed, and he was aware of just how foolish that had been.

Even more foolish, he wanted to do it again. Wanted to hold her against his side and make sure whoever hurt her couldn't get near. Wanted to inhale the scent that was uniquely hers and hold it deep in his lungs as he lay claim to every inch of her body.

Their eyes locked together, every thought seeming to broadcast between them in a single stare.

She looked away and he shifted in his seat. "You're safe here, Gemma, and you're welcome to stay as long as you want, no strings attached."

Tell me you want strings.
Tell me you want to be in my bed.

She didn't look up. "Thank you."

He gestured to the other side of the loft. "There's a guest room next to the bathroom. It has walls and everything."

"Do you mind if I shower?"

"Go ahead. There are towels in the closet."

"Do you have something I could wear?"

"Sure."

He dug through his dresser while she showered, listening to the running water as he picked out sweats and an MIT T-shirt, imagining how she'd fill it out and telling his hard-on in no uncertain terms she wasn't interested in fooling around tonight.

Instead, he needed to get back to working on Royce's laptop, and he poured himself two fingers of scotch before settling into a sleek leather recliner and getting down to business.

The first thing he did was run a search for Gemma Faraday in Royce's email. The only hits were for some political fundraiser they were both invited to attend.

That was a relief.

He selected all of the fundraiser emails and marked them as read. Just over five thousand more to go. At this rate, it might take him a week just to find the threatening emails.

A small balloon popped up in the top corner of the desktop. REMINDER: MONTHLY PASSWORDS EXPIRE IN

FORTY-EIGHT HOURS AND REQUIRE TWO-FACTOR AUTHENTICATION.

"Oh, fuck."

He pinched the skin between his eyes. Without Royce's cell phone to receive a password reset code, Logan would be unable to log-in after the next two days.

The clock was ticking.

11

Logan's towels were bigger than Gemma was, and she thought she might get lost in the one she was drying off with. It smelled like him and she brought the soft fabric to her nose, inhaling his scent and sighing.

So he was a decent guy, offering her shelter from the storm without expecting anything in return. After the night they'd spent together, the air between them was sizzling with unspoken questions, and she suspected he'd be interested in having sex again if it was a possibility.

Last night you were drunk.

Today you wouldn't have any excuses for sleeping with a guy half your age.

Not half, exactly, but certainly younger.

And he worked for HERO Force. Ethically she was skating on ice so thin she could see fish through it. She bit her lip, remembering the smelly man on top of her her and his threats. There would be no recusing herself now.

She was scared, and that fear drew her to Logan. She

forced the thoughts of her attacker out of her head and focused on the man outside the bathroom door.

She was so aware of him and his proximity, his body so sculpted and physically so fit she could squeeze his muscles and shout for joy. She eyed her naked self in the mirror, the tattoos that swirled around her reconstructed breasts reminding her she was far from a blank slate.

She was a woman with a history, and it was stamped on her as clear as day for anyone to see if she let them get close to her. Reaching up, she ran her finger along the petals of a flower.

The room had been dark when they'd made love.

Had sex.

You had sex, Gemma. You didn't make love.

But it had felt like that to her, which was ridiculous.

Her eyes dropped and she finished drying her body. He hadn't seen her scars, hadn't had that chance to judge whether she was still a real woman. She squeezed her eyes shut.

Of course you're still a woman.

Even more so, for all she'd been through.

She wrapped the towel around her body and opened the door, cool air sweeping across her skin as she made her way to the guest room. There were clothes on the bed that smelled like Logan too, and she dressed in them, the fabric like an intimate caress, keeping her warm.

She came back out, spying him under a modern lamp, typing on a computer. With his glasses he looked older, more distinguished. He looked...

Sexy.

And damn it all, she liked him. He was the kind of man she could have a relationship with, assuming she could stomach the age difference.

The first stirring of need rumbled through her belly. He was offering her sanctuary, which made her feel protected. Cared for. She walked toward him, her mind opening to him as she moved closer. Maybe it didn't matter how old he was. He was a man, not a child. A man who seemed to want her just as much as she wanted him.

When she stood just outside the circle of light, he lifted his head and met her eyes.

"Better?" he asked.

She nodded. She was suddenly unsure of herself, and she swallowed against the tightness in her throat. "Are you working?"

"Yes."

"Okay. I'll just grab my blanket." She spun on her heel and took the afghan, anxious to beat a hasty retreat.

"Wait."

She kept walking. "I'm going to get a glass of water and head to bed," she called over her shoulder. She reached the kitchen and hung her head, pulling the blanket tightly around her middle.

He spoke from right behind her and she jumped. "What is it?"

"Uh, where do you keep your glasses?"

He reached into a cupboard and handed one to her, but didn't let go when she would have taken it. "Since I first saw you standing in the rain, I've wanted to kiss you. Do you know that?" he asked.

Her thighs squeezed together. "You have?"

He nodded. "But I needed you to understand you could stay here, even if you didn't want to be kissed." He touched her uninjured cheek. "So you need to tell me if you want me to kiss you or if I'm crossing a line you'd rather keep intact."

"Screw the line."

He reached for her just as she went up on her tiptoes and kissed him. Her hands went around his neck and held him to her, his tongue teasing and exploring her mouth. He put the glass down behind her, knocking it over on the stone countertop, the glass clamoring.

Gemma dropped the blanket.

He pushed her back against the kitchen counter, his hips pressing against hers as he continued his skillful assault on her mouth.

And skillful he was. She never would have guessed the young stud with the MIT T-shirt would be such a passionate lover, so sure of himself and in tune with her desire.

He trailed kisses down her neck as his hand slipped beneath her shirt, gently cupping her naked breast, and he groaned. He squeezed her, his hand taking in the full shape.

Oh God, he's looking for my nipple.

A nipple she didn't have anymore.

She squirmed away from his seeking hand, suddenly uncertain. Unlike their first night together, the room was light enough for him to see her body clearly, and she was suddenly terrified of what he would do when he saw her chest.

"You okay?" he said huskily.

No, she wasn't okay. This was a moment that should be easy and natural, but she was stuck with a body that looked anything but ordinary.

Fuck you, cancer.

She wasn't going to let that damned disease take another thing away from her. "Wait." She grabbed the hem of the shirt with both hands and pulled it over her head in one swoop, baring herself to him from the waist up and holding her breath.

The cancer had taken her breasts. Rather than try to replicate her old chest, she'd chosen an elaborate series of tattoos that flowed from the corner of her underarm across the swell of each breast.

They were the most personal part of her body. They represented her fight. Everything she had gone through.

Her will to live.

Those tattoos were her spirit itself, and now she was exposing them to this man, not knowing if he would be repulsed or accepting, and her chest squeezed tightly as she waited for his reaction.

He wasn't touching her. He wasn't saying anything.

He stared at her, his face unreadable as his eyes trailed over every inch of her decorated skin. She exhaled shakily. When she couldn't stand his silence any longer, she moved to put the shirt back on.

"Wait, I'm not done."

He traced a line as it swirled around the crest of one breast. "There are flowers and designs I don't understand, but there are also symbols. I found the silhouette of Justice."

Her mouth pulled down hard at the corners. He wasn't disgusted. He was in *awe*. "She's blindfolded."

He stroked her gently. "And an ocean wave with the sun setting in the background."

There was a heart there too, for the child who would never play on that beach, but she didn't need to tell him that. Most of the designs were too personal for anyone else to understand. She hadn't created them for anyone but herself.

"So beautiful." He bent his head and kissed each breast tenderly, reverently.

She lifted his face to hers and kissed him, knowing she

was very much a woman in Logan's eyes, feeling sexier than she could remember feeling in her lifetime. Her hands slipped beneath his shirt and she lifted it over his head.

"Go get a condom," she commanded. "I have a blanket, and this time, we're doing it on the floor."

12

Gemma sat up in bed with a start, her heart pounding. It took her a moment to remember where she was, the familiar shapes and shadows of Logan's apartment coming into focus.

She'd had a crazy dream about the man who attacked her. She smelled the stench of his filthy skin before he knocked the wind out of her, following her to the ground as the full weight of his body landed on her back.

She'd tried to scream, but it came out as a whimper. "Leave me alone!"

A man's shiny black dress shoes stepped in front of her face. "I love you, Gemma." It was Royce's voice, but when she looked up to see him, she was staring into the eyes of her father.

"Does anybody need a lawyer?" he asked.

She shivered. No way she was ever going to get back to sleep tonight.

Logan shifted in his sleep and she looked back at his sleeping form. The two nights they'd spent together had been the best two nights she'd had in a long time.

It's not like this can turn into something serious. You're way too old for him.

She frowned. Some women had relationships with younger men. Why couldn't she?

She wrapped Logan's bathrobe around herself and padded to the living area. The sun would be up soon, the eastern half of the sky already illuminated, throwing the loft into some kind of twilight.

She wandered around the space, considering the sparse furniture and decor. In a way it gave the few pieces he had that much greater significance, and she imagined she could get to know the man by the things he used to fill his space.

One wall held a bookcase, desk and several framed degrees. The PhD in computer science came as no surprise, but the medical degree had her mouth hanging open. She touched the abrasion on her cheek. He hadn't thrown in a sly, "I'm a doctor" when he'd treated her injury.

Perhaps the degree was a joke, like a fake magazine cover or a prank lottery ticket. Something you could print off the Internet to amuse your friends.

Or maybe it isn't.

She hummed softly. She might have to change her computer-nerd-with-the-body-of-a-Greek-god idea of him if it was real. She focused on the year he graduated and gaped, doing some quick mental math.

She was thirteen years older than him, not quite as bad as she'd thought, but seeing the year in print was a reality check.

Her hip bumped the desk in front of her, a computer monitor coming to life from the movement. Her eyes went back to the big screen, which was mirroring the open inbox on the smaller laptop.

The names of several judges caught her eye, along with a political figure she knew professionally. Was this her email she was looking at?

She narrowed her eyes, scrutinizing the names, one standing out from the others.

Barbara Royce.

It took a minute for confusion to give way to understanding. This was Royce's computer, not her own, and those were emails to his wife. She looked back at Logan, his eyes closed, his naked body tangled in the bedsheets.

He was just a guy she'd met in a club.

Or was he?

She'd simply assumed theirs was a chance meeting, but what if it was not? The kidnappers knew who she was—one of them had attacked her on the street.

Oh God. What if another one had approached her in a nightclub?

Pure fear blew through her like the coldest breeze. Logan was connected to the people who'd taken Royce. He must be.

He was dangerous.

She was in danger.

As if on cue, Logan's eyes opened. "Hey. Good morning." He sat up, looking from her to the computer screen and back again. "What are you doing?"

She looked to the door on the other side of the apartment, but she'd have to run right past the bed. "Nothing."

He threw back the covers and stood, the nakedness she'd found so alluring now frightening her. "Why are you on my computer?"

"It's not yours." She grabbed a pair of scissors from a cup on the desk, holding them like a sword. "It belongs to

Anthony Royce. Now how about you tell me why you have it?"

"I'm not going to hurt you, Gemma."

"Shut up. You lied to me."

"No, I didn't."

"You let me think you were just some stranger. But that's not true, is it?"

"I'm just going to grab my shorts." He pulled them up, zipping the zipper and leaving the button open so they hung low on his hips.

She'd taken one look at that body and hopped into bed with him. What a fool!

"Tell me how you're involved with Royce. Did you take him?" she demanded.

"No. He's a client of HERO Force. I met him the day he was kidnapped. The explosion happened right in front of our headquarters." He held up his injured palm. "I tried to save his wife, but it was too late."

His burned hand.

She'd wondered about that.

"What a saint," she said. "But you still didn't explain how you managed to hook up with me. Don't tell me it was a coincidence. I don't have my idiot blinders on anymore."

"I followed you and your friend there." He walked slowly toward her. "I went to the scene of the explosion. I watched his wife die hours earlier and I was upset. I was just...walking."

He was almost to her, and the hand holding the scissors started to shake.

"Then there you were, and I followed you and your friend to the club. I wanted to know who you were. How you knew Royce."

He went to touch her shoulders and she jerked her body out of reach. "Don't touch me."

His stare spoke volumes, reminding her of every intimacy they'd shared, that a touch now was nothing compared to what they'd already done together. She'd all but begged him to make love to her last night, actually letting herself think it might be the beginning of something real between her and Logan.

Stupid girl.

"I'm telling you the truth, Gemma. I want to help you."

He moved so quickly, she barely registered the movement before he'd lunged and taken the scissors from her hand. "You don't need these. I would never hurt you."

She pushed past him, feeling herself tremble. "I'm going home." She gathered her clothes from the floor, holding them tightly against her chest.

"You're not safe there anymore, remember?"

"Call me crazy, but I don't feel so safe here, either." She went in the bathroom and slammed the door behind her before twisting the lock and leaning up against it.

All she wanted to do was hide. She should have known better than to get involved with a total stranger.

Walk the straight and narrow.

Don't do anything reprehensible.

No casual sex.

Expect everything to come out in the open, and when it does, know that you will be able to hold your head high.

She dressed quickly, desperate to leave this place. She'd be safe in her own apartment, doors and windows locked against the masked man who'd attacked her and the unmasked one who'd crawled beneath her skin.

That was what she got for relying on a man to save her,

instead of saving her own damn self. She opened the door and kept her head high as she passed him, not meeting or stare.

"Please don't go," Logan said.

She slammed the door behind her.

13

Hawk had a funny feeling about this that had nothing to do with invading someone's privacy. He sat behind Royce's desk in his home office and began opening drawers.

"This place is off the hook," said Austin. "Can you imagine how much money this guy must have?"

The house was easily five thousand square feet, and every room looked like it had been professionally decorated. Hawk had just started looking at houses online, imagining buying one with Olivia, so he had some idea of what a place like this might cost.

Millions.

State judges must get paid pretty damn well.

Or else they didn't.

"The house doesn't bother me as much as the family," he said. "Those girls didn't want us here, permission or not."

"You got that too, huh? Though I think the older one kind of liked me." Austin looked up from the filing cabinet he was flipping through and winked at Hawk.

"I'm pretty sure she had something stuck in her eye." He

closed one drawer and opened another. "Well hello, Ruger." He pulled the revolver out of the desk drawer. "Loaded."

"What kind of dumb shit leaves a loaded gun in a desk drawer?"

"The state justice kind of dumb shit, apparently."

"Hold the phone, here's something interesting." Austin pulled a file out of the cabinet. "A bank account in Switzerland. People actually have those?"

"Sure. You don't have to put your name on it. It just has a number. Good place to hide money. What's the balance?"

"Just over three million."

"Maybe our judge is a saver."

"Yeah, right. That's probably it. I'll bet he started when he had a paper route as a kid."

Hawk dug through paperclips, perfectly sharpened pencils and sticky notes. A cigar box was tucked into the back of one drawer, and he pulled it out, opening it on the desk. Inside was a photograph of a beautiful young woman, topless in bed.

She was looking at the camera, a sly smile on her face.

"Something tells me this isn't Barbara Royce." Hawk held up the picture for Austin to see.

He whistled. "That's not what she looked like in the wedding picture on the wall downstairs, that's for sure. Flip it over. See if there's anything on the back."

"Nothing."

"Maybe it's part of his secret stash. Don't all guys have some porn hidden somewhere?"

Hawk fingered the picture. "I don't think this is porn. The way she's looking at the photographer... I think she loved him."

"An affair?"

"It's possible." He tucked the cigar box back into the

drawer, minus the photograph, which he stuck in his shirt pocket.

The men worked quietly for some time.

"I think I found something," said Austin. He brought a folder to the desk and opened it in front of Hawk. "You recognize any of these names?"

Hawk scanned the list. "No. Should I?"

"My sister was in charge of fundraising for the art gallery downtown. A lot of these names sound familiar. I think they're donors."

"For an art gallery? What does that have to do with Royce?"

"Rich people usually like to spread their money around. They don't just give to the art gallery. They give to charities and causes."

"And politicians. Let me see that." Hawk flipped through the folder. "Do you think it's possible Royce was misappropriating campaign funds from his elections?"

Austin looked around the room. "Judging from this house, I'd say it's fucking likely. Rich people are always hiding something."

"You got something against people with money?"

"Hell yeah. Most of them got it by doing something wrong. Think about it. Honest work doesn't pay so good."

"Some people are born into money. They just manage to keep it."

"Exactly. You give your average working Joe a million dollars, what's he going to do with it?"

Hawk grinned. "Give a lot of it away."

"That's right. You buy your mama a house, you buy your nephews and nieces each a car. But rich people don't think that way. They don't have the same morals. And I'm pretty damn sure my pops never had a picture of half-naked woman in a cigar box somewhere."

"You don't think poor people cheat on each other?"

"Not the way the rich folks do," said Austin. "That's what I liked about the SEALs. They've got high moral standards. They don't let the riffraff in, know what I mean?"

"I don't know about that. The day Cowboy got his swim fins, he almost missed the ceremony because he was buying weed from an AWOL buddy and banging the chaplain's daughter in the officer's barracks."

Austin laughed. "I really like that guy, Cowboy. He's all right."

14

Cowboy scratched the beginnings of a beard as he took in their surroundings. "This looks just like my uncle Jake's place. He lived in the mountains of West Virginia, hunted deer and made moonshine. Near as I can figure, he never did have a job."

It had taken them nearly an hour to get here, leaving the staples of civilization in their dust long before.

"You don't have to go far to end up in the middle of fucking nowhere," said Jax.

Piles of dog excrement littered the property, the air ripe with the smell of shit baking in the sun. "Got a guard dog around here somewhere," said Cowboy. He looked at Noah. He'd barely said two words since they left headquarters. "You ever seen the backwoods of Georgia?"

"No, but I saw Deliverance."

"That counts," said Jax.

Stewart Cole's property was just over nine acres between a fundamentalist church and a one-truck volunteer fire station. Piles of junk were strewn about the property. A pile of radiators, another of metal lawn chairs.

"Must be a scrapper," said Cowboy as he started toward the house. The one-story dwelling was made of a patchwork of materials, from a metal and wooden roof to a cinder block porch that seemed to have been an afterthought.

"I'm guessing he's collecting the steel," said Noah. "My money's on prepper."

"There going to be a great demand for rusted radiators and mid-century lawn chairs at the end of days?" asked Jax.

Noah grinned. "It's the metal. Some of them use it to make their own weapons. Others think of it as currency. Owning steel means they'll be able to produce their own goods."

"How do you know this shit?" asked Cowboy.

Noah hooked his thumbs in his pockets. "It makes good sense to be prepared."

"You telling me you've got a hundred radiators stashed someplace just in case you need to pound out your own quarters?"

"I'm ready for the day when our supply system can no longer meet the needs of American citizens, if that's what you mean."

Cowboy narrowed his eyes. "I knew this other guy who was obsessed with the end of the world. Events he couldn't control, that kind of shit. You want to talk about a prepper, this guy was off the hook. Had himself completely convinced weather patterns were all fucked up because of people's influence on the earth, and the world was going to become covered in water from all the rain."

Noah sighed heavily. "Let me guess, he built an ark, right?"

"You two know each other?"

Noah shook his head. "Asshole."

Cowboy grinned. "What are there, like meetings or

something where you guys socialize? Because I'd like to get in on that shit."

"Shut up, Cowboy," said Jax.

"I have some lawn chairs I could bring," said Cowboy. "Extruded aluminum. I was thinking I could make my own tinfoil when all the Shop-Quiks close down."

"Joke all you want," said Noah. "But someday you're going to come knocking on my door because you weren't prepared for a disaster."

"Maybe so." The wind kicked up, blowing dust into Cowboys face. He stopped and squatted down, running his hand along the dirt in the driveway. "Doesn't look like anyone's been here in a while. No tire tracks in the driveway since the rain."

"It rained yesterday," said Noah.

"Not here, it didn't. They had several inches in a downpour before the heatwave, but nothing since. The dirt here is smooth. It hasn't been driven on since the storms."

Jax's voice was low. "Keep your weapons handy, just in case. This guy isn't exactly our best friend."

The last hundred yards of the walk to the house was in the wide open, making Cowboy grateful for his bulletproof vest and gun. Stewart was suing them for killing his brother. He was unpredictable, at best.

"I'll go in first," said Jax. "Noah, you go around back in case he tries to leave."

"I thought we just said he wasn't home," said Noah.

Cowboy shook his head. "We said nobody's come or gone in a vehicle. I didn't say squat about him not being home."

They walked under the front porch eave and Cowboy exhaled loudly. If no one had taken a shot at them as they crossed to the door, he figured it was less likely they would do so now.

Jax knocked. "Mr. Cole?" He knocked again, yelling louder this time, "We'd like to talk to you."

"You just trying to make sure he has enough time to grab his gun?" whispered Cowboy.

"Shut up." Jax turned the knob on the door and opened it a crack. He eyed Cowboy. "Do you find it strange that a prepper would leave his door wide open?"

"Most of these guys have locks up one side and down the other," said Noah.

Cowboy held his gun at the ready as Jax kicked open the door with his foot. The offending odor of decay hung on the air, slamming Cowboy in the face like a blow.

Jax went to the left and Cowboy went to the right, holding his gun at the ready as he checked for anyone inside. He rounded the last corner in the kitchen, he and Noah holding their firearms at each other. They both put them down. "Clear," Cowboy yelled.

"Clear," Jax yelled from the other side of the house.

"What the fuck is that smell?" asked Noah.

"That would be dinner." Cowboy gestured to the stove, where a rotting carcass of a small animal sat in a pan. "Looks like a groundhog. You know, when the shit hits the fan you're going to wish you had that. Want me to wrap it up for you to-go?"

Noah ignored him. "It was left as a present for any company that might wander inside."

"Come here," called Jax. "You've got to see this."

They found him in tiny room that opened to a bed with filthy blankets and a stained pillow. But it was what Cowboy saw next that made his muscles twitch.

The walls were plastered with photographs and clippings, his eyes instantly drawn to a picture of himself and Charlotte. "Holy Christ." He crossed to it, plucking it from the wall as he clenched his jaw.

There were pictures of Jax too, along with one of Jessa driving her car with the window down. But the worst was a snapshot of a baby lying in a crib.

Oh, fuck.

Cowboy looked at Jax. "Is that your daughter?"

"Yes."

"We have to get this guy." Every muscle in Cowboy's body was pumped and ready to attack. Cole was after his family. That's what these people were. His brothers in arms. His sisters. A child who might as well be his niece, and the woman he loved more than anyone. "This shit just got personal."

Jax's face registered no emotion. "Dead, Leo. He needs to be dead. Just like his brother."

Cowboy's eyes shot to Noah's. If he'd heard Jax, he gave no indication. Noah simply turned and moved to a second wall, this one covered with clippings of a different sort. "Is this the brother?"

Cowboy turned around. "That's him all right."

NAVY SEAL KILLED IN FREAK ACCIDENT.

The paper was yellow with age.

LOCAL SOLDIER WITH PTSD DIES AT SHOOTING RANGE.

Noah took a step back. "I'm going to check out that footlocker."

Cowboy moved closer to a framed picture, Garrison Cole stared back at him in his dress blues, the American flag in the background. The last time Cowboy had seen those eyes, they'd been staring at the sky, lifeless.

I didn't mean to do it.

Call 9-1-1.

I thought she was older.

"Holy shit," Noah's voice brought Cowboy back from the past. "We have a problem."

Cowboy turned around. Inside the military footlocker at the end of the bed was a red LED timer counting backwards.

Fourteen seconds.

"It's a bomb!" he yelled. "We must have tripped something on our way in. Get the fuck out. Now!"

The men ran out the door, across the cinderblock porch and into the blinding sunshine. The explosion threw them through the air, everything in slow motion, and Cowboy wondered at that moment if Royce was somewhere inside that cabin. Had they killed him just by looking for him?

Cowboy landed hip-first, sliding from the force of his own momentum like he was stealing third base, his mouth full of dust. He spit on the ground and looked around at his teammates. "Well that was fucking close. I hate bombs."

Jax groaned. "You're an explosives expert."

"Won't keep my ass from getting blown to bits when my number's up." He got to his feet. "Trick is to kill this fucker, first. This shit just got personal."

15

Logan sat in a captain's chair in the rear of the HERO Force van, two monitors glowing in front of him. One feed was from the camera trained on Gemma's brownstone. The second was from a camera pointed at her street, where he was parked.

Both were equipped with night vision.

He'd be damned if he was going to let anything happen to her because he'd scared her away. Someone attacked her right here not twenty-four hours before, which meant they knew where she lived and she certainly wasn't safe here.

She was angry with him. That's why she'd come home.

It had been easy to find out where she lived, as the only lawyer named Gemma in the greater Atlanta area. Even without a listed phone number he'd tracked her down with a single Internet search. He'd have to teach her the finer points of existing anonymously in the information age, especially after this experience.

Assuming she ever speaks to me again.

He opened Royce's computer and it came alive with a small song. From the messages he'd already read, he knew

Royce had a very busy docket, a doting wife, and an account on Tinder that told Logan the other man wasn't everything he seemed to be.

Logan was down to fewer than a thousand messages left to read, but his brain's ability to multitask could be a curse. He could still see Gemma in his mind's eye, remember what she felt like beneath him. She'd wanted a night of wild sex, and he'd given it to her.

Then you gave her another.

But that wasn't the problem. He liked her. He liked her a lot.

Movement on a monitor caught his attention. A woman's silhouette appeared in the upper right corner window.

Gemma.

His stomach clenched. For a moment he let himself wish things were different.

He shook his head, forcing his thoughts back to the computer. Campaign contributions. A gubernatorial dinner invitation. Airline reservations to Maui for Royce and his wife. An email from someone named, "Old Friend."

Logan narrowed his eyes and clicked on it.

You've been living on borrowed time, and I just called in your loan.

Logan highlighted the sender and filtered the inbox, looking for more emails from this person. It came up with fifty-six matches.

The first set the tone for the rest.

I saw you in the paper the other day, getting an award for your years of faithful service to our community. They think you're a hero, but I know better. You let guilty men go free, and you will pay for it.

Each email was another commentary on Royce's supposedly shady character and the fact that he'd been bought and sold instead of issuing justice when it was due.

Each of you swore allegiance to this country. You from safely behind a bench like the coward you are, my brother from the battlefield. But when he needed you to speak up for truth on his behalf, you abandoned him, let his killers go free, and you will pay.

This sure sounded like the HERO Force case, and Garrison Cole's brother Stewart was looking more and more like the sender.

He leaned back in his chair, wishing he'd been privy to all of Royce's conversations with Jax and Cowboy. Logan knew what he wanted to search for next. He opened the filter window and typed JAX.

His fingers hovered over the keys. If he had a question about Jax's communications with Royce, he should just ask. But that wasn't what he was going to do.

He hit enter.

A short list of emails popped up on the screen and Logan clicked the most recent, sent from Royce to Jax the day before the explosion. It was just a few lines long.

Someone has been sending me emails threatening my life. He knows.

He says if I don't make it right he is going to kill me. Have you two received anything like this? He doesn't mention your names directly, but he alludes to knowing you are involved on some level. We need to talk. I'd like to do this in person. Are you free this week?

"Holy shit." His eyes skimmed back over the passage, looking for the two words he needed to read again. *He knows.* Jax and Cowboy were just as guilty as he feared.

Movement on the monitor caught his attention—headlights coming toward him down Gemma's street. It was a pickup truck, and it pulled to the side of the road two cars behind Logan.

This area was a mix of commercial and residential properties, but they were right at the end of the block on a Sunday night. From the location of that truck, he could only be heading to one building—Gemma's.

Logan cursed under his breath as he ran through his options. The HERO Force van was completely blacked out. The man in the truck wouldn't be able to see he was in here. He grabbed his tactical duffel bag and quickly changed into dark camouflage before moving back to the monitor.

He zoomed in on the cab of the truck. A man was clearly visible, fat and middle-aged, and looking through binoculars aimed at Gemma's apartment.

Logan considered his options as he called Austin for backup. He could walk over there and ask the bastard what he was doing. He wouldn't get an answer, but he'd surely scare the other man away. Unless he was really bad news, in which case he might have a weapon.

What he really needed was to get a plate number and warn Gemma. The night vision camera picked up on the reflective material of the license plate, making it appear completely white. He'd have to get the plate number the hard way.

As Logan watched, the man leaned forward, peering at Gemma's apartment. Logan clenched his jaw. He couldn't wait for backup. It was go time.

He opened the monitor app on his smart watch and selected the view of the truck driver, dimming the brightness to its lowest level. He grabbed his holster and weapon and flipped a switch, throwing the interior of the van into darkness before carefully sliding open the van door.

His vehicle shielded him from the driver's view, so long

as he didn't catch the other man's attention by rocking the van.

He crawled on his hands and knees, fisting his left hand to protect his burned palm as he moved past the car that separated him from the pickup truck.

It was too dark to see the plate number. He stopped and withdrew his cell phone, taking a picture he hoped he could enhance later.

The sound of a gun being cocked made his head snap up, half expecting to see the weapon trained on him. His heart stammered, but the man was nowhere to be seen.

Logan tapped his watch, the screen coming to life. The man in the truck pulled a ski mask over his face and opened his door, the squeak in Logan's ears matching the image on the tiny screen.

Logan pulled out his Glock.

He could clearly see the man's feet as he walked to the front of the vehicle. Surprise was his ally, and Logan launched himself at the man, clocking him in the head with the butt of his weapon.

The man lost his footing but recovered quickly, trying to train his gun on Logan. In a split second Logan had to decide whether to fire or attempt to disarm the other man.

His leg came up in a roundhouse kick, sending the firearm flying. The metallic click of a switchblade registered on his consciousness. The man swung at him, and in a reflex action Logan held up his hand to defend himself.

The blade sliced into his already burned palm. Pain blossomed, hardening his reserve. He trained his sight on the other man and fired.

The man's eyes widened and his hand went to what was left of his ear. He turned to run and Logan grabbed him from behind. They were locked together, wrestling for control, the smell of blood and putrid sweat hanging on the air between them.

Logan was slammed against the cab, his skull bouncing so hard on the metal his vision blurred, the man now more a shadow than anything. Logan's knee came up hard, catching the man in the balls and doubling him over.

The truck door opened and Logan wrestled to keep it shut.

He gripped his gun tightly.

Shoot him.

He hesitated.

Shoot him now.

The man made it into the truck and the door started to close. Logan's left hand shot out, the steel frame of the door and truck body cracking the bones in his fingers.

The truck started, Logan barely getting out of the way before the tires peeled over his feet.

He stared at the blurry taillights as they drove out of sight, self-rebuke taunting him. He should have pulled the trigger. His knees started to give out and he forced himself to walk.

Gemma.

The stairs to her front door were a mountain. He squeezed his eyes shut, trying to clear his vision. He used his right hand to guide himself up them as he cradled his left hand against his chest.

He rang the bell.

The sound of footsteps on the stairs and the light came on overhead. "What are you doing here?" She gasped. "Oh my God, what happened to you?"

"I got in a fight with the guy watching your apartment. Lucky for you, I was watching it, too."

16

Gemma wrung the bloody washcloth out in the bathroom sink and exhaled a shaking breath.

Logan's hand was badly cut and bruising in the same area he'd burned trying to rescue Barbara Royce. It made her stomach turn to look at it, but nonetheless she cleaned it and bandaged him up.

Thank God he was here.

What would have happened to her if he hadn't been?

She'd foolishly felt safe once she'd reached her apartment and bolted the door, but Logan's account and injuries frightened her to the core.

She clearly remembered the helplessness she'd felt when the man had tackled her on the sidewalk. She'd been stupid to push it from her mind so easily.

She found the supplies Logan had asked her to gather and returned to him at the kitchen table. Two of his fingers were broken and he guided her through splinting them.

"Are you really a doctor?" she asked.

"MD and a PhD. You can call me doctor doctor."

She smirked. "Like that song."

"What song?"

Her face fell. "It was before your time, I guess." She finished taping his splints in silence. "Tell me why you had Royce's computer."

"He gave it to HERO Force. Someone was sending him threatening emails and he wanted to know who it was."

"When was this?"

"The day he was kidnapped. It happened right outside HERO Force headquarters."

"Which is why you were there, and tried to help Barbara."

"Yes. I'm sorry I didn't tell you I knew Royce. It was work. It didn't seem right to tell you."

She met his stare. "You want complete honesty from me, but you filter your own story."

"I won't do it again."

She released his hand. "You're as good as new." It wasn't true. Not even close. He'd been hurt protecting her, and she felt that truth like a debt. "I shouldn't have come back here," she said.

"You were angry."

She shook her head. "I was scared. I didn't know if I could trust you."

"You believe me now?"

"Yes."

"Then no more secrets. Tell me what they want from you."

She bit her lip. Her attacker had been very clear. She wasn't to tell anyone.

Logan leaned forward. "You're safe now, Gemma. I'll protect you."

She believed he would. He already had. "He wants me to

throw a verdict. To convict, no matter if the evidence supports it."

"Isn't that up to a jury?"

"Not if the men waive their right to a jury trial, which they have."

"The men?"

She met his stare head on. This was the hardest part, and even as she spoke the words, she prayed she wasn't killing Royce. But she needed help. She couldn't figure this out on her own. "I'm the judge assigned to the HERO Force case. The men the kidnapper wants me to convict are your coworkers, Jax Andersson and Leo Wilson."

"Oh, fuck."

"And if I don't do it, Royce will die."

He pinched the skin between his eyes. "When does the trial start?"

"Tomorrow."

"Damn it. Can you postpone?"

"I might be able to stall, but not for long. The suit was filed months ago by the brother of the deceased."

"Are you going to find them guilty?"

She shook her head. "I don't know. I'm holding out hope the evidence will prove they did it."

"They're men of integrity."

"You're saying they're innocent?"

Logan only stared at her.

"I'll have to make a decision when it's time for my verdict." She stood and moved to the sink, picking up the dish soap and squirting some onto a sponge. "I certainly can't do it now."

Her voice sounded meek and she hated herself for her own weakness. One way or another, she was responsible for the fate of three men, and she suddenly wondered if she was capable of making such a judgment.

Logan walked up behind her and hugged her. "It's going to be okay. We'll find him."

She frowned, her mouth pulling down hard at the corners. "And if you don't, I'll have to decide who lives and who dies. I could be disbarred. No, I should be disbarred for even considering this."

"Shh." He kissed between her shoulder blades.

"And you. What am I doing with you? You work for a company that's being sued in my courtroom. I'm practically old enough to be your mother."

"Not quite."

"Close enough. You're thirty-one. I'm forty-four."

"The age difference doesn't bother me."

"You're not the one everyone would refer to as old."

"Hey." He turned her around to face him. "I like you. I think you like me, too. There's something good between us."

She lifted wary eyes to his. "It's just sex."

"It could be more, if you wanted it to be."

She sighed. "I'm sorry, Logan. This isn't going to work. You must see that. And even if age wasn't a factor, I can't deal with a relationship right now. Not in the middle of the worst few days of my life."

He nodded. "Come on. We need to go back to my place. It isn't safe here."

She hung her head and covered her eyes with her hand. She didn't trust herself at his apartment, but knew he was right.

"You can have the guest room," he said.

"Okay. Now I just need to have enough resolve to actually sleep in it."

17

"Come on, you son of a bitch, show me what you've got." Logan changed the resolution parameters on the computer program. He'd scanned in the photo of the license plate from the truck outside Gemma's apartment, and was trying to get his computer to sharpen the image by making smart choices about the next pixel in line. So far, all he'd gotten was fuzzy gibberish.

Without that plate number, he had no way of learning who was watching Gemma.

She was sleeping in the guest room after an especially quiet drive over to his apartment, and he was doing his damnedest not to think about her.

Why did it bother him so much that she didn't want to date him? He already had her attention in bed. Did he really need her to say she wanted more from him?

The problem isn't sex. The problem is you want to hold her while she's sleeping almost a much as you want to fuck her senseless.

He sighed loudly.

He was pathetic.

With fast fingers he copied the image layer and tweaked the algorithm again, as if solving the license plate problem was as good as solving the problem of Gemma.

Lots of women liked younger men, but she seemed to think his age was a liability. His eyes went to the guest room door which had been closed for the better part of an hour and a half.

Clearly, she wasn't coming back out to tell him she'd changed her mind, and could she please sleep next to him tonight. He pulled his eyes back to his computer screen and made more minor adjustments, copied more image layers.

He stayed awake until his eyes were crossed just staring at the screen, because that way he could put off making a decision about Gemma tonight.

He stood and put his hands on his hips, staring at the guest room door for a long moment. "Fuck it." He took off his glasses, plugged in the computer so it would keep working, and pulled his shirt over his head.

He rapped lightly on her door.

No response.

He tried the handle, pleased to find it open, and crawled in bed behind her. He put his arm around her midsection, the smell of her freshly-washed hair surrounding his face.

He could tell the moment she woke up, her body stiffening. "If you want me to leave, just say so."

She threaded her fingers through his, her body relaxing once more, her breath deepening until he thought she was asleep.

"It's too easy to like you," she said quietly.

He nuzzled her back, inhaling her scent through his T-shirt. "It's too hard to stay away from you."

"I meant what I said, Logan. I can't deal with a relationship right now."

He reached around her middle and cupped one breast. "You said it was just sex."

She hummed lightly and arched her back, her ass pressing against his pelvis. "Yes, but you disagreed."

"I was wrong." He kissed her neck. "I take it all back."

She giggled and rolled onto her back, looking up at him. "Isn't that convenient."

He shifted, moving his leg between hers. "It is." He kissed her lips and hugged her body, her skin toasty warm from sleep. Her hands touched his chest and moved up to his arms, kneading his muscles.

She lifted her face to his and kissed him. "Just for tonight."

He nodded. "Whatever you say."

She was soft in all the right places and he sunk into her flesh with his mouth and hands. When his body joined with hers the world seem to still, and he knew there was no way one night with this woman could satisfy his need for her.

She was fierce. She was strong. She was gentle and weak, and he would do anything in his power to keep her by his side.

18

Gemma clasped her hands together, clammy and cold. She was standing at the closed door to her courtroom, unable to cross the threshold. Dizzy, she leaned against the wall.

On the other side of that doorway the trial of her lifetime awaited, and it had nothing to do with the case. She was being tested, her commitment to the law coming face-to-face with her concern for another human being.

She turned the doorknob, propelling herself into that other dimension before she could stop.

All rise.

She made her way to her seat behind the bench and sat down. Could they see what she was going through? The stress that threatened to crush her, that nearly stopped her breath?

The bailiff was speaking. Gemma's eyes finally lifted to meet those of the defendants, Jax Andersson and Leo Wilson. Logan called him Cowboy. They looked like military men, fit and trim with short hair and steely faces.

Men with integrity, Logan said.

Unlike herself.

She wanted to be sick.

It's not too late. You can call the FBI and put a stop to this miscarriage of justice before it begins.

But there was another man to consider. Royce's life hung in the balance, and one wrong move could cause his abductors to kill him.

Please don't let it be glaringly obvious that I've been corrupted. Please let there be at least some convincing evidence of their guilt.

The lawyers began opening arguments. They went by quickly, and Gemma felt like a passenger on a roller coaster going down a steep hill with no power to stop the ride.

But you can stop it.

All she had to do was speak up.

What about Royce?

He was a judge himself, one of the highest in the state. He of all people would sympathize with her dilemma. She imagined Royce in her predicament. What would he do in the same situation?

All you have to do is interrupt the proceeding.

She picked up her gavel, her fingers gripping the wooden handle tightly. It felt foreign, somehow strange beneath her hand and she turned it in her palm.

Crudely engraved into the wooden handle were three words.

WE'RE WATCHING YOU.

She dropped the gavel as if she'd been burned. She stood. The prosecutor abruptly stopped talking. A hush fell over the room.

Her eyes scanned the courtroom, going from face to face. There were too many people, too many sets of eyeballs staring back at her, and at least one of them was a monster.

She found her voice. "The court will take a short recess." She rushed to her chambers, slamming the door behind her like she'd narrowly escaped Hades itself.

She was hyperventilating, her lungs taking in more air than she knew what to do with. She bent at the waist and grabbed the couch, pulling herself onto it.

There was pounding on her chamber door and terror flashed through her. Had she locked the door behind her when she came in? "Who is it?"

"Logan."

She rushed to the door and opened it a crack. Her secretary wasn't at her desk, thank goodness. "What are you doing?" she bit out. "You can't be seen talking to me."

"What happened back there? You looked like you saw a ghost."

Her eyes went from side to side, then she pulled him into her office. "They got to the bench. I don't know how. The room's always locked when court's not in session, but somehow they got to the bench. My gavel was engraved—somebody scraped it out with something sharp—and it said, 'we're watching you'."

She heard herself tripping over her words, knew she was barely making sense.

"Just now? That was written on your gavel?"

She nodded quickly, a noise that was half sob, half laugh escaping her mouth. "What do I do? They're out there right now, in the courtroom."

"Maybe. Or else they just wanted to scare you into thinking they were there."

"Well it worked, okay? They scared me."

He touched her upper arms and she pulled away. "Not now. Please don't touch me."

"Call off the rest of the trial for today. You're not going to make it back out there like this."

"I said we'd take a short recess."

"So pick up the phone and tell them you changed your mind. You're not feeling well. Anyone who saw you in that courtroom will believe it in a heartbeat. Then you're coming with me to HERO Force."

"I can't do that! What if the kidnappers see me?"

"We'll just have to make sure that doesn't happen." He pulled his polo shirt over his head. "Take my clothes."

"Have you lost your mind? You're a gangly six-foot-God-knows-what man, and I'm a short little woman."

"Just put it on."

She did as he said, unzipping her robe and hanging it up on a hook.

"Lucky for you, I'm wearing shorts today," he said, stepping out of them and handing them to her.

"If your shorts fit me, I'm going to kill myself."

"I have a belt."

She fastened it around her waist. "I look ridiculous. I certainly don't look like a man."

"Hard to look like a guy with that rack." He winked at her. "But you look a lot less attractive than you usually do. Do you happen to have a hat?"

"Bottom right desk drawer."

He pulled it out, reading, "Happy Seventieth Birthday Judge Hollurman." He handed it to her. "Put your hair up."

She did as he said. "You're standing in my chambers in your underwear."

"You like?"

She gestured to his feet. "Maybe without the socks."

He smiled. "Next time."

"What are you going to wear?"

"I was thinking your robe would look pretty fantastic on me."

Her eyes widened. "You can't wear that. Everyone in the building will look at you and realize you're not one of the judges."

He shrugged. "So I'll claim to be a singing telegram guy. I'm certainly not *old enough* to be a judge."

"I hate you right now."

"You look terrible."

"Where am I going?"

"The Ferrari's parked in the west lot. The keys are in your pocket. I'll be twenty feet behind you, hot stuff. Now, lead the way."

19

Gemma had a sickening feeling in the pit of her stomach as the elevator made its ascent. Up until now she hadn't technically done anything wrong, but this car was about to open on the threshold of the point of no return, and she had little choice but to cross it.

Logan took her hand. "You'll be safe here."

"I know." She was grateful there was someplace she could go. The elevator slowed and stopped, the door opening. Too bad she had to sacrifice her career for her own safety.

They stepped into the HERO Force lobby, dramatic lighting and sleek designs in the carpet making Gemma feel like she'd just walked onto a movie set.

"Jax here yet?" Logan asked the man at the reception desk.

To his credit, the receptionist didn't bat an eye at their outfits. "Yes, sir. He just got back."

"Great." He held his palm on a pad on the wall and opened a door, holding it for Gemma to precede him. He moved beside her and led the way, past offices and a glass-walled room filled with computers and monitors and a large panel of lights and buttons along the side. It looked like some high-tech control room, making her think of *War Games*.

No point in mentioning that reference to Logan.

"Maybe I should just lie low in a storage room or something," she offered.

"Jax and Cowboy need to know you're here."

They rounded one final turn and a man's voice could be heard speaking in clipped, even tones in the distance.

"Let me change my clothes, at least."

He stopped. "Okay. There's a ladies' room right over there."

She changed quickly and rejoined him, the man's voice she'd heard before getting louder until Logan pulled her inside the room it was coming from.

Jax Anderson was standing, a telephone to his ear. His eyes met Gemma's, recognition like a spoken accusation. "Let me call you back," he said, replacing the receiver.

"Gemma Faraday, Jax Anderson," said Logan.

"You're the judge from court this morning."

"She needs somewhere safe to stay," said Logan.

Jax frowned. "This isn't a shelter."

Gemma touched Logan's arm when he would have spoken. "Someone's trying to hurt me. Someone related to Anthony Royce's kidnapping."

Jax's eyes shot to Logan. "Explain."

"I was guarding her apartment when I was attacked by a man, clearly there to do her harm."

"What were you doing guarding her apartment?"

"We've been seeing each other," he said. "She was

attacked on her street yesterday, but insisted on returning to her apartment last night. I was concerned."

Jax narrowed his eyes at Gemma. "Dating coworkers of defendants, Your Honor? You realize that's a conflict of interest."

She raised her chin. "There are extenuating circumstances that make it impossible for me to recuse myself."

"Go on." Jax crossed his arms. "If you're seeking protection under my roof, I'll need all the information."

Gemma looked to Logan, who nodded. She licked her lips. "The man who attacked me told me to find you and Leo Wilson guilty, or Royce will die. They said they'd kill him if I told the authorities."

She felt like Jax was looking through her, as if he could see every truth and lie she'd ever spoken, and she bristled beneath his assessment.

"What can you tell me about this man?" he asked.

"Nothing. It was dark. He tackled me from behind. All I remember is the body odor. Then in the courtroom today, 'we're watching you' was scraped into the handle of my gavel."

"That's why you hightailed it out of there."

She nodded. "That's when Logan suggested I come here."

"Have you told anyone else?"

"No." She thought of the news footage of the burning car with Barbara trapped inside, and she bit her lip. "I was too scared."

"One last question, Judge Faraday. Who is Anthony Royce to you?"

Gemma felt her face heat. "We're both judges, though in different courts. I see him at political functions, mostly."

"I mean personally."

From the corner of her eye she saw Logan turn toward her. A knot formed in her throat and she considered what to say. "We had an affair eight years ago. I wasn't aware he was married at the time."

Logan's voice was heavy with disappointment. "Why didn't you tell me?"

"I was ashamed. It was in the past. I didn't think it mattered."

"It matters to the kidnappers," said Jax. "They knew you would try to save his life."

She laughed without humor. "If anything, I'd be more likely to kill him myself."

Jax sat behind his desk, touching the fingertips of one hand to the fingertips of the other. "You can stay in the empty office at the end of the hall. I'll have my secretary take care of whatever you need. Logan, I'll see you in the conference room for the briefing."

"Gemma should be there."

Jax nodded. "Fine. Bring her along."

Gemma followed Logan out of Jax's office. He didn't talk to her or turn around. He entered a small room with a desk and a file cabinet, waited for her, and closed the door behind her.

He was angry.

She was sure of it.

She licked her lips. "I'm sorry I lied to you about Royce and me."

He moved close to her back. "I'm putting myself on the line for you. Will there be any more surprises?"

"No."

"Good. I don't like surprises." He whipped her around

and kissed her, taking her mouth like he had every right. One arm held her tightly against him while the other fisted in her hair, pulling her head back. All she had to do was open herself to him and he did the rest, plundering her mouth with his own.

20

Logan pushed her back against the wall. He needed this, needed to remember how she felt in his arms, surrendering to his kisses.

All he could see was her flushed face as she admitted to having an affair with Royce. Feel his own embarrassment. He could see her body beneath that old man while Royce humped her with what Logan could only imagine was his long, skinny dick.

What had a beautiful woman like Gemma ever seen in that guy? Royce was powerful, sure. But he was so much older it made him question her interest in him. How could one woman be attracted to one man so much older than her, and another so much younger?

She'd only ever claimed to want sex without strings. Now you're surprised to find out you're not her type?

Damn it. His cock was rock hard with the need to have her, even as he was aware of the meeting in a few minutes down the hall. She grabbed his ass and squeezed his cheeks, making the decision for him. He growled. "We have to hurry."

She lifted her shirt over her head and he picked her up, taking her to the desk and lifting her skirt, yanking down her panties and pulled them down her legs as he unzipped his fly, releasing his aching erection.

There wasn't time for foreplay and he didn't want any. "Tell me you have a condom," he ground out against her mouth.

"In my purse." He handed her the bag and she dug frantically through it, cursing before finally withdrawing the foil packet.

Logan sheathed himself and thrust inside her with one powerful push, finding her wet and swollen for him. They fucked quietly, their breath and the whispered sounds of pleasure the only sounds in the room.

But it wasn't enough. He needed to dominate her, show her she belonged to him, purge the image of her and Royce from his mind once and for all. He pulled out and flipped her over. "I want to spank you."

"Yes," she whimpered.

He slapped her ass cheek with his open hand. "You should have told me." He pushed inside her, fucking her hard.

"I'm sorry."

He slapped her again. "Do you like that?"

"Yes."

"Don't lie to me again."

"I won't. I promise." She clenched rhythmically around his shaft and he came in a powerful rush of sensation. When he was through, he pulled out, noting the bright red handprints on her ass cheeks.

His handprints from hitting her.

"Turn around," he said. He kissed her again, loving the way she obliged him. "You're a good match for me."

She untangled herself from his body, pulling away and putting her clothes back on. "We have good sex."

"It's more than that, and you know it."

"The age difference—"

"You didn't care when it was Royce."

Her face colored, her cheeks now matching her ass where he'd hit her.

"That was different."

"No, it's not."

She didn't meet his eyes. "You've got your whole life ahead of you, Logan. The last thing you need is to be saddled with me when you should be looking for a relationship with someone your own age."

He closed the space between them and tilted her head up. "And if I want a relationship with you?"

"I'd say it's just sex."

"It could be more if you'd let it."

"Well, I'm not going to, so that's that."

He crossed his arms. "You're full of shit. You know that? Why won't you even consider it?"

The last thing she needed was to fight with him about this. "I'm trying to protect you. Don't you see that? I want you to find someone you can actually have a future with. If you and I get serious…"

"Then you get scared?"

"No." She met his stare head on. "I'm a dead-end street, Logan. I'm thirteen years older than you. Thirteen! I can't have kids. There's no point in dating me. You have to see the logic in that."

He narrowed his eyes. "You can't have kids?"

"I've had chemo and radiation, some of the strongest drugs they make. I'm infertile."

"There are other ways to have kids."

"You don't even know me! This is a pointless conversation. I don't want to date you. End of story." She turned her back to him and faced the window, her arms crossed over her chest.

He suspected she was crying.

He stared at her back, wishing he hadn't pushed the issue. She was beyond stressed. "Gemma, I'm sorry."

"We shouldn't do this anymore. I told you from the beginning I only wanted something physical, but you just keep pushing."

"We have a spark—"

She spun around. "You're not listening to me. I don't want to go out with you."

Damn it, she was right.

From that very first night she'd been honest with him, but the more he grew to like her the more he kept trying to change her mind.

The problem wasn't Gemma.

It was him.

"I appreciate what you've done for me, Logan. I don't want to know what would have happened if you weren't outside my house the other night. But I think it's best if we end things now, before they get out of control."

His lips hardened into a straight line. "There's one more thing I forgot to tell you. The computer finished analyzing the license plate from the van outside your apartment. They're government plates from a state vehicle kept in downtown Atlanta."

Her mouth dropped open.

He nodded. "I'll see you in the briefing."

21

Logan closed the door too loudly when he left, making Gemma jump. She understood why he was angry. She was angry, too.

She'd gotten a glimpse of what her life could have been like without cancer, like a child spying the brass ring on the carousel, but it was permanently out of reach. She could never be the woman Logan wanted. She could never give him the things he so flippantly dismissed as unimportant now.

But what about later, when the resentment kicked in? She knew exactly what it was like to think you'd make your peace with something inherently unfair, only to rally against it like a prisoner pulling against his chains.

She wouldn't do that to Logan.

Not now. Not ever.

He didn't know what she knew, couldn't imagine the depths of that suffering he was so eager to take on. No, he'd find someone else, probably even one day soon. He was right at that age when so many men settled down and got married, even started a handsome young family.

Her eyes burned and she cursed her own weakness, refusing to let the tears fall as memories of her thirties came to mind. She'd been a bridesmaid and an honorary aunt more times than she could count.

"Stupid girl," she mumbled under her breath. She wiped at her eyes, ensuring they were dry, then bent and picked up the condom wrapper from the ground, surprised to see it was the one April had given her at the dance club. That meant she and Logan had used the old one from her purse that first time they were together.

She shrugged. Surely old protection was better than no protection at all.

She made her way back to the glass-walled conference room and sat beside Logan. Cowboy nodded, letting her know he'd already been updated as to her presence at HERO Force.

Jax began. "After the bomb that exploded at Stewart Cole's house, I think it's safe to say he's involved in the kidnapping of Justice Royce. He had hundreds of pictures of Cowboy and me, along with our loved ones, and a virtual shrine to his brother, Garrison."

Cowboy spoke. "For those of you who are not aware, Garrison was a member of HERO Force who was killed in a training exercise six years ago. Jax and I were charged with murder in Garrison's death. Justice Royce dismissed those charges for lack of evidence."

"Now civil charges have been filed, charging Cowboy and me with the wrongful death of Garrison." Jax gestured to Gemma. "Judge Gemma Faraday here is the judge assigned to that case."

"Whoa." A big man across the table held up his hands. "What are you doing here?"

"And you are?" she asked.

"Austin Dixon."

She nodded. "I was contacted by Royce's kidnappers. They want me to find Mr. Wilson and Mr. Anderson guilty, regardless of the evidence against them."

Austin turned his head and looked at her sideways. "She's not supposed to be here."

Logan cleared his throat. "Judge Faraday needs our protection. She's part of this mess, and an apparent target for Cole. We're taking care of her."

Gemma's shoulders dropped in relief. Her eyes went around the room to each of the men—strong, capable soldiers.

"Cole's house was a trap," said Jax. "He knew we'd find it. Now we need to figure out where he's really hiding Judge Royce."

"Does he own any other property?" asked Austin.

"Negative. No living relatives, either."

"Friends?"

"Everything we've got on this guy says he's a loner," said Logan, flipping through papers in front of him. "Lives in the woods. Unemployed and on public assistance for a psych disability. If he had friends, they would have been few and far between."

"A hotel, or rental property?" asked Jax.

"Possibly." Logan rubbed a finger along his jawbone. "But there was no Internet service at the cabin. Cable lines don't reach out that far and he didn't subscribe to any of the satellite options."

"Then a rental's probably out," said Austin. "All that shit's done online these days."

Gemma leaned forward. "What about Royce's property?"

Logan shook his head. "We already checked the house."

"He has a house up on Lake Hartwell, or at least he used

to. There's a peach orchard, too. It's been in his family for generations."

The men looked around at each other.

"Would you be able to find this place again?" asked Cowboy.

"I don't know. I don't think so. It was just up a hill from a gas station, but I don't know the address."

Logan opened a laptop computer. "Searching property records now. Do you know if it was passed down on his side or his wife's?"

"He talked about spending time there when he was a kid. It definitely belonged to his family."

The click of Logan's fingers on the keys was fast and furious. "Got it. Eighteen fifty-four West Lake Road. Property of Anthony and Barbara Royce."

"Nice work," said Jax. "Let's roll."

Hawk leaned forward in his chair. "Hang on a second." He was staring at Gemma. "I found a picture when Austin and I were searching Royce's home office. I believe it's a picture of you, Judge Faraday."

She shrugged. "What kind of picture?"

One look at his face and she knew exactly the picture he was referring to. Royce had taken it at a hotel in the Adirondacks shortly after they'd started seeing each other, claiming he wanted something racy to keep in his desk.

Her cheeks filled with heat. "Oh."

"Oh!" said Austin, pointing at Hawk. "I know what you're talking about. You put it in your pocket, didn't you?"

Jax cleared his throat. "Return it to her."

Hawk hesitated.

"Go on," Jax said.

Hawk put it facedown on the table and pushed it toward her.

"Now let's get going," said Jax.

Gemma stood up and tucked the picture into her pants pocket.

"You're staying here," said Logan. His voice was sharper than normal, and she knew he'd been embarrassed by the photograph, and her knowing about Royce's lake house. It was clear to everyone in the room she'd had a relationship with the missing judge.

"But I've been there before. I might be able to help."

"You might be in the way or get yourself killed. I think you should save the trip down memory lane for another time."

"That's not fair." A couple of the guys turned around, but she held her ground. "I'm sorry if my past embarrasses you, but I should come with you on this trip. No one else here knows the property like I do. I could be useful."

"I'm trying to protect you," Logan said.

"And you will protect me. I'm not afraid to go up there because I know you'll keep me safe. I'll stay in the car. Whatever you want me to do."

"We're taking the chopper and the van," said Jax.

Gemma rolled her eyes. "Then I'll stay in the van, but don't leave me sitting here by myself when I could help find Royce."

Logan put his arm out, gesturing for her to go first.

"Thank you."

"Stay in the van."

"I already said I would."

22

Heat lightning danced in the evening sky as Logan ran through the orchard surrounding Royce's lake house. The smell of rotting fruit clung to the humid air, pungent and cloying. His breath came in rhythmic pants, adrenaline intensifying his senses.

Noah's voice came through Logan's earpiece. "I've got eyes into the house."

"Any sign of Royce?" Jax asked on the shared com channel.

"Negative. Two tangos so far, both male."

"Where are you?"

"Fifteen feet up a tree on the north side of the front door. Clear shot into the kitchen and master bedroom, over."

Logan was approaching from the far side of the property, still a considerable distance from the house. "Jax, you got audio inside?" he asked.

"Negative. There's some kind of interference. I'm going to get closer. Austin, what's your location?"

"I made it through the orchard on my side and took

cover behind the shed. I can hear yelling from inside the residence."

"Yelling for help, or in anger?" asked Logan.

"Anger."

Logan crested a small hill, the lake house coming into view, rising above the orchard. He stayed low. He could see Austin's shed and wondered where Jax was.

Cowboy's voice was loud in Logan's ear. "Charges placed under the tango's van. Payback is a bitch, gentlemen."

"I'm going in," said Jax. "The backdoor to the house is unlocked. Somebody get over here and cover my six."

In the distance, Logan saw the slightest movement by the backdoor of the house, knowing it was Jax in camouflage.

"Right behind you," said Austin, his form moving low from the shed to the house.

Noah's voice was calm. "You two stay away from the windows. I've got a clear view of the kitchen sink area if you need me to take the shot."

"Stand down," said Jax.

"Approaching the house now," said Logan, staying low and seeking cover behind an oak tree some twenty yards from the back door.

"Definitely arguing," whispered Jax. "Three voices. We may have more than two tangos. What can you see, Noah?"

"Two men in the kitchen, both wearing black."

"Can you see their faces?"

"Negative."

The sound of breaking glass reached Logan's ears. He needed to get closer to that house in case Jax took a shot.

What do you mean in case?

Jax always takes a shot.

"Don't shoot unless you're sure it's not Royce," said Logan.

"Don't piss into the wind, either," said Cowboy.

Logan rolled his eyes.

"And look both ways before you cross the damn street, kids."

Logan's earpiece exploded with yelling voices. A shot rang out in the distance.

"Tango has his back to the wall, rifle in plain sight. The other one's missing," said Noah.

From the cacophony in his right ear, Logan was pretty sure tango number two had found Jax.

"I'm going in," said Logan. "Austin, on my six."

"You've got it."

"Now, Noah," said Cowboy.

The sniper's rifle echoed through the orchard.

"One down," said Noah. "Looking for number two."

Austin snapped in Logan's ear. "Doc! Up high!"

Logan looked up a split second before a man jumped from the second-story window, his boots landing on Logan's head, twisting Logan's neck as he fell.

Austin fired, but the man kept going.

"He's heading to the van," said Logan.

"Stay back," said Cowboy. "Arming the charges. Preparing to detonate."

The man got into the van and closed the door. It exploded in a blinding flash of light, the noise deafening and flaming debris flying everywhere.

Logan covered his head, the shock wave knocking him against the house.

"Inside. Go! Go! Go!" yelled Cowboy.

Logan ran toward the back door just as a propane tank

on a gas grill exploded. When he opened his eyes, the house near the grill was on fire, completely blocking the doorway.

"Jax!" he ran toward the front of the house, looking for another way in.

"He was in the kitchen, fist-fighting a tango," said Cowboy.

Jesus.

How many people were in there, and where the fuck was Royce?

"Hurry, Doc. He's getting his ass kicked."

The front door was locked and Logan smashed a window, carefully climbing in over the broken glass, the thickly knit fabric of his fatigues resisting the sharp edges. The inside of the house was quickly filling with smoke and a piercing chemical smell.

He covered his mouth with his arm and ran, looking for the kitchen. He came full circle. "Where the fuck is the kitchen?" he yelled.

"Upstairs. Second floor," said Noah.

"You could have mentioned that."

"Jax is down and the tango is out of sight. Repeat, I can't see the tango. You've got to get Jax out of there."

Logan's eyes were burning from the smoke as he made his way up the narrow staircase, not knowing where the enemy was hiding.

"Shit!" yelled Austin. "The fire shot up the dumbwaiter. Hallway's completely blocked. I can't get to Jax."

"I've got him," said Logan. "Get out of there, now. This place is going up way too fast." He reached the top of the stairs and crawled to stay beneath the worst of the smoke. "Which way is the kitchen?" he yelled into his mic.

Out of nowhere, he was hit in the back of the head with

something heavy and solid. "You're gonna die, you son of a bitch, just like my brother."

Stewart Cole.

Logan made out the silhouette of the man just as an object came swinging toward him again.

A baseball bat.

He ducked just in time, the barrel clipping him on the skull, and trained his weapon on Cole.

He fired three times in quick succession, the other man falling to the ground. Logan moved close to Cole's face, seeing life still lingering in his eyes. He didn't even hesitate, shooting him point-blank in the forehead.

"Jax!" Logan screamed, crawling past Cole's body and through a pool of blood. His lungs filled with noxious air, the heat of the hallway way past a hundred degrees.

In his earpiece he heard the voices of his HERO Force brothers, their words incomprehensible over the roar of the blaze.

He made it to the end of the hallway.

No kitchen. He'd gone the wrong way.

He turned back the way he'd come, an eerie orange glow now visible through the smoky haze. He crawled through Cole's blood, it's metallic odor mingling with the burning air that was taking his breath away.

It was getting hotter with every inch he crawled in that direction, and he struggled to hear what his teammates were saying.

Had Jax made it out safely without him? Was he attempting a rescue that didn't need to be made?

"I'm not leaving you behind," he ground out against his clenched teeth. "Jax! Can you hear me?"

He rounded a corner and the flooring changed from wood to vinyl. The smoke was lower here, visibility no more than a few inches beyond his face. He put his belly on the floor.

There, through the thinnest layer of clean air, he could see Jax's leg across the room, unmoving.

With a burst of renewed energy, Logan crawled to him, quickly moving to his friend's face.

He was unconscious.

Logan's lungs were screaming, pain unlike any he'd ever known seeming to turn their lining to something caustic. He looked around for a window. A doorway. Some way out of the room.

I'm not going to make it.

Fire broke through the floor beside Jax's head and Logan wrapped his arms around Jax's torso. He remembered Noah's words.

Stay away from the windows. I've got a clear view of the kitchen sink area if you need me to take the shot.

Logan's eyes snagged on the drainpipe coming down from the old farm sink behind Jax's head. The window must be on the opposite wall.

He pulled Jax away from the flames and pushed him toward the window. The legs of a chair came into his field of vision and he grabbed it, hurtling it toward where the window must be.

Glass shattered and cool air rushed into the room, feeding the quickly growing flames. They billowed high against the wall and he reached for Jax's frame.

Again he grabbed Jax and lifted him into his arms, forcing his body to a stand against the intense blowing of outside air into the fire.

"Over here!" he called out the window, his eyes so stung he couldn't see.

Austin's voice in his ear was like the sweetest music. "We've got them! Out the kitchen window!"

What happened next was a blur of motion as HERO Force rallied to get them down. Then Austin was on a ladder, pulling Jax from Logan's arms.

"Climb down the ladder, Doc." It was Cowboy, calling as if from so far away. Logan listed dramatically to the side. Dizziness overtook him and he fell back into the smoke and heat.

Cowboy's voice was the last thing he heard before he blacked out. "I'm coming for you, buddy. I'm gonna get you out of there."

23

Vitals are stable, pulse is elevated. Minor burns and external injuries—scrapes and bruising. Pulse ox is rising, currently at eighty-five.

The smell of smoke clung to Logan like a campfire as he worked to make sense of the voices hovering over him. He must be on rounds in the hospital.

Someone had been in a fire.

He remembered the dead weight of Jax in his arms, felt the heat of the flames so close to his body. His eyes shot open just as the ambulance doors closed.

"Breathe deeply, sir," said the EMT, a bald man with dark brown skin trying to fasten an oxygen mask over Logan's ears.

Logan pulled it off. "Where's Jax?" he croaked.

"The other big guy? Dark hair?"

Logan nodded.

"Already on his way to the hospital. I hear you saved his life."

Logan leaned back, allowing the man to put the oxygen mask on him. He remembered crawling on his hands and knees, searching for Jax. He remembered firing a bullet into Stewart Cole. He remembered arguing with Gemma.

She didn't want to see him anymore.

The ambulance started to move. Logan sat up suddenly. "Wait!"

"Sir, you need to—"

"Where's Gemma?"

"I don't know who Gemma is, sir."

"Stop the ambulance."

"We need to get you to the hospital."

Logan pulled the mask completely off his head and ripped an IV out of his arm. "I said stop it, now." He cleared his throat and immediately regretted the action as the raw sides of his trachea rubbed against one another. "I need to get out. I have to make sure she's okay." He turned toward the driver. "Stop this vehicle, goddamn it!"

The ambulance came to a stop. Logan stood and wrestled with the door until it opened. Five hundred feet away stood Cowboy, and Logan took off at a jog. "Where's Gemma?" he asked.

"Back at headquarters. She didn't come with us."

"Yes, she did. She was in the van with Jax."

Cowboy's eyes went wide. He and Logan ran across the property searching for the vehicle parked on the other side, a full moon lighting the way.

If she'd gotten hurt because of him, he'd never forgive himself.

Logan reached the van before Cowboy. Gemma was slumped over in the passenger seat, what looked like dark stains all over the upholstery in the light of the moon. Logan opened the door and she fell into his arms, lifeless.

Blood.

Those stains are blood.

It was splattered along the back of the seat in a pattern that was all-too familiar from his medical school days. "She's been shot! Get that ambulance over here!"

Cowboy took off running.

Logan rested her on the ground and felt for a pulse. It was weak and racing. "She's in hypovolemic shock. She's lost too much blood." He didn't know who he was talking to.

He didn't care.

He lifted her shirt and saw two wounds, one on the edge of her breast, the other just below her rib cage. The lower was bleeding far more than the upper and he folded her shirt, using it and his hands to put pressure on it.

"You're going to be okay." He stared at a drop of blood as it rolled down her breast and around to the side of the other, seeming to mix into the tattoo of the ocean wave where it touched the shore. She'd been through so much already. It didn't seem fair she should be dying right in front of his eyes.

"Please let her be okay," he begged.

The ambulance came racing across the property, headlights shining and emergency lights flashing. Logan showed the EMTs her wounds and stepped back so they could care for her, strapping her onto a gurney, loading her into the back, and taking her away—leaving him and Cowboy standing in the dark outside Anthony Royce's burned down lake house, in an orchard full of rotting peaches.

Crickets chirped in the distance.

"You know what this means?" asked Cowboy.

"What?"

"This isn't over."

"What do you mean?"

"You killed Cole, Noah got one from his sniper's nest,

and I got one when the van exploded. That's three tangos down."

"But someone shot Gemma."

"That's right. Someone shot Gemma, and this ain't over yet."

24

Logan refused to be admitted, spending the night in a corner of the Intensive Care Unit, half sleeping in a chair next to Gemma's still form. He awoke every time a nurse or doctor came to check on her, and each time they gave him a sad little smile.

She's going to make it.

He knew she would.

Jax had almost died from smoke inhalation. When they pulled him from the building, there was soot in his mouth and he was coughing up blood.

Hell, at least he was coughing.

A few more minutes inside and he wouldn't have been doing that.

Logan didn't envy Cowboy making that call to Jessa, and he wondered if this would be the straw that ended Jax's time with HERO Force completely.

Jax had stayed two nights in the hospital and gone home. Gemma was still there.

One bullet had punctured her lung, another her diaphragm. She'd had emergency surgery and a ventilator was helping her breathe. But Logan's biggest worry was her level of consciousness.

He just wanted her to wake up.

She'd sustained a head injury in addition to the gunshots—though no one knew from what—and her brain was swollen.

She was so damn still, the beeping of the machines and the whoosh of the ventilator the only noises coming from her bedside. He crossed to her and brushed the hair from her forehead.

He never should have let her come to the orchard. She would have been safe back at headquarters, but he'd allowed himself to be swayed by her lobbying, telling himself she'd be okay.

It was foolish, and it had nearly gotten her killed.

"You're going to go out with me after this. I don't care if I have to drag you out in public with me. You're going."

I love you.

There it was again, the emotion he had no right to be feeling. He'd only known her a few days, but he suspected he would feel that way about her for the rest of his life—even if she chose not to be in it.

And she might not.

"Maybe I won't drag you."

God knows, she didn't even want to date him before all this. It wasn't very likely she'd change her mind because he'd nearly gotten her killed.

His stare took in the bandages over her chest and shoulder. With a bullet wound only inches from her heart, she was lucky to be alive.

And I'm lucky to have her.

But he didn't have her. Not really.

She'd come to him looking for sex, but for him, it had

become more than that. He cared about her, wanted to spend time with her after she was well, and not out of some sense of obligation.

She was sure to push him away. Hadn't she already done that, zeroing in on the age difference between them and pointing out all the things he could never have with her?

He wanted kids one day, sure. But if he and Gemma were meant to be together long-term, then he knew there was a family meant for them as well, even if it wasn't the regular kind. It didn't matter where they came from.

Four days later she was moved to her own private room. Logan was still there, having only taken short breaks to eat, sleep or shower.

It was pouring rain outside the window, the deluge pelting the glass as he rested his forearms on the metal bar of her hospital bed. The room smelled like disinfectant, the walls covered in sheets of textured plastic. He'd had too much time over the last few days to examine their repetitive pattern.

A white-haired nurse came in and took Jemma's vitals. "Are you the father?" she asked.

Logan furrowed his brow. "No. Her father's in a nursing home."

"Not her father. The baby's father."

He furrowed his brow. "What?"

The nurse's eyes opened wide. "Uh...the doctor told me the baby's father was in here. I just assumed that was you."

"No."

Her cheeks flushed a deep crimson. "Please, don't tell anyone I said anything. Patient privacy is important in this hospital. I could lose my job."

"It's okay. You have the wrong room. She can't have kids."

The nurse looked at the chart in her hands and back to Logan. "Gemma Faraday."

"Yes."

She dropped her eyes, closing the chart as she reached for the rolling blood pressure machine.

"Wait. Is she pregnant?"

"I'm so sorry, sir."

"Because you shouldn't have said it or because it isn't true?"

She was halfway out the door.

"Do you have any idea how much this means to me?" he called. "What if she is pregnant, and she never tells me herself? What if she makes a decision because she thinks I don't love her, or that she's too old for me? Maybe it wasn't a mistake you came in here."

The nurse stopped walking and faced him. She held up the chart. "A patient's medical record is strictly confidential. I made a mistake here today." She turned and placed it in a basket on the blood pressure machine, then pulled it into the hallway and walked away.

Logan stared at the blood pressure cart, Gemma's chart sitting right inside the wire basket. Either that nurse was a real idiot or one hell of a softie.

He stepped into the hallway and looked from side to side. No one paid him any mind. He took the chart back into Gemma's room and opened it, his eyes scanning the information.

His heart squeezed in his chest.

HGH levels consistent with day eight of pregnancy.

A wide smile broke out on his face. He was going to be a father.

25

Gemma's head was pounding and her throat was more sore than it had ever been in her life—one from the concussion she'd sustained, the other from the breathing tube that had kept her alive for the last week.

And then, as if reports of her coma-like state weren't shocking enough, the doctor dropped a bomb on her she hadn't seen coming. She was pregnant.

Pregnant!

She couldn't stop crying. She cried all the way through a visit from the governor's secretary, who told her she had just lost her job. And while they were reserving the right to disbar her pending a full investigation, initial indications were that she would get to keep her law license, which she knew damn well she didn't deserve. They should've taken it all, stripped her of everything.

That would've been justice.

But she'd been granted mercy instead.

She had no idea how they'd found out about her conduct on the HERO Force case, and frankly she didn't care. She didn't even have the desire to defend her actions. Nothing mattered beyond the new life that had taken hold in her battered, war-torn, forty-four-year-old, cancer-free body.

She was going to have a baby.

It was a miracle.

It wasn't supposed to happen. It wasn't even supposed to be a possibility, yet here she was, knocked up.

She laughed through her tears. She was pregnant with Logan's child. She knew exactly when it happened, desperate for him to make love to her and drunk out of her mind, she'd grabbed the wrong condom from her purse, using her old one instead of the one April had given her.

She rested her hand on her abdomen, laughter and tears turning into emotional sobbing.

"Gemma?"

She jerked her hand away from her stomach and wiped at her eyes. "Logan."

He looked tired but good, concern clearly ironed into his features, and she wondered how much time he'd spent at the hospital with her. A nurse had rushed to call him when she awoke, and he'd made it here in less than an hour.

"Are you okay?" he asked.

She wiped her face. "Yes."

"God, I'm glad to see you awake." He leaned down and hugged her, gently kissing the top of her head. "I was worried sick."

"Good as new." Her voice was raspy and she put a hand to her throat.

"It's from the ventilator. It will feel better in a day or two."

She nodded.

"What did the doctors say?"

"I had a hole in my lung and another in my diaphragm. They stitched me up and I seem to be doing well."

"Is that it?"

She cocked her head. "And a concussion. My head hurts."

And I'm carrying your child.

She grinned, the expression feeling absurd on her features, like she was a crazy person trying to keep a secret.

He was looking at her intently.

"They said I should be able to get out of here tomorrow or maybe the next day. How's Royce?"

Logan nodded. "Good. His wounds were mostly superficial. Twenty-five stitches and an aspirin for the road. He positively identified Stewart Cole."

"Thank God he's all right."

He sat down. "Did you see who shot you?"

"No. I was sitting in the van with Jax. He was trying to use that parabolic listening device to hear inside the building, but it wasn't working. Some kind of interference, so he decided to get closer."

"And what did you do?"

She shrugged. "I stayed in the van, I guess."

"You guess or you remember?"

She furrowed her brow. "I'm not sure. The next thing I really remember is..."

Finding out I was carrying your child.

"...waking up here," she finished.

"We need to make sure we got everyone. Three of the kidnappers were killed at the scene, including Cole. But no one saw any of them leave the lake house and head toward the van where you were."

"So you think there might be another one out there."

"Right."

A chill ran up her spine.

"You can stay with me, if you'd like," he said.

That was the last thing she needed. "No. That's all right. You've done enough already."

She saw the unspoken questions in the depths of his eyes, but she wanted some time to think. It would be difficult to do that with him there.

"I can put a security guard on your doorstep," he offered.

"That might be nice. Just for a while until I get my sea legs back under me."

He took her hand and kissed the back of it. "You scared me, Faraday. Made me think about how much I like having you around."

Her stomach clenched. "I need some time, Logan."

"Take a few days if you need them, but I want to see you again. Don't keep me waiting too long."

26

Sweat ran down Logan's face and into his eyes, but he didn't stop punching the speed bag. He needed this release, this physical outlet for all the emotional shit pent up inside him.

He could see the way Gemma touched her stomach, the look of awe on her features before he walked into the room. But once he stepped inside, her hand flew away and her expression became shuttered.

She didn't want him to know she was pregnant.

He punched harder, the speed bag coming faster with each swing. Maybe she was telling the truth and she just needed some time to think.

God knows he did. But she knew about the baby and chose not to tell him, which made him fear she had no intention of telling him at all.

Was she going to keep it?

She was career focused. She didn't plan on having any kids because she didn't think she could have any. He couldn't assume that an unplanned pregnancy would change any of that, no matter how much he wanted to believe it would.

The muscles of his shoulders were burning and he pushed himself harder, needing to feel something besides the pain of this lingering doubt.

Should he give her space, give her some time to think? Or should he go over there and tell her how he felt, tell her he desperately wanted her to keep their baby. Keep her in his life.

Cowboy walked into the gym. "First you train on AK-47s, then basic explosives and martial arts, now this. What's next, Doc? You going to earn your swim fins?"

"I don't need to be a fucking SEAL. You fools would be dead in the water without me." He hit the speed bag with a burst of force that left it flying in his wake.

This conversation with Cowboy was long overdue. He'd been avoiding it for so long, but now it was just another avenue to release the stress inside him—a punching bag he could hit. "If I'm going to stay with HERO Force, some things need to change."

"I'm listening."

"I may not be a SEAL, but I bring a lot to the table and I'm sick and tired of being treated like a fucking kid. That isn't how you and me are going to work. Either you open your eyes and acknowledge that I'm goddamn useful around here, or I'm off the team."

He was ready for a fight. Ready to force his hand, ready for battle. Or he'd walk away if this son-of-a-bitch couldn't see he was worthy.

Cowboy narrowed his eyes. "Maybe you're right."

"You bet your ass I'm right."

"I'm not used to you being on the front lines. I'm not used to you being capable."

"I was always capable, Leo. I just hung back and let you guys patronize me, because I thought you were better than me. But those days are done. I looked up to you, but now I know that's bullshit, and I'm not willing to work for a company that thinks I'm less-than everybody else."

Cowboy stared at him for what seemed a long time before reaching out and touching his shoulder. "It's about time, Doc. I've been waiting for you to stand up for yourself, though I've got to say, I didn't understand I was part of the problem. I'm sorry about that."

"It's all right."

"We'll make some changes."

Logan nodded, wiping away the sweat from his eyes. "Good."

Jax walked into the exercise room. "Question for you, Doc. Where does Cole's death leave the lawsuit? Does it die with him?"

"Legally, it passes to his heir, but I don't think he has one. If that's the case it will be dismissed."

Cowboy screwed up one side of his face. "You know way too much shit."

"That's why he's a good guy to have around," said Jax. "Well, that and saving my ass from a burning building."

"Doc here wants more responsibility," said Cowboy.

Jax turned and walked away, calling over his shoulder, "About fucking time."

Cowboy looked at Logan with a smirk. "Told you."

Logan shook his head and went back to punching the speed bag. "You guys are fucking nuts."

"You want to tell me whose ass you're kicking over there, Doc?

"Not especially."

"Faraday seems like a real good woman."

Logan glared at Cowboy, who pretended not to notice.

"Something happen between you two?" Cowboy asked.

"I have an idea," said Logan. "How about you and I discuss the finer points of your relationship with Charlotte?"

Cowboy turned on his heel. "Never mind."

"Hang on there, brother. I think this is a fine idea. You've been dating my sister for what, almost six months now?"

"Seven."

"And she moved in with you about a hot week after the cruise."

"Yep."

Logan got his rhythm going again, the speed bag bouncing hard between its platform and Logan's alternating fists. "Guess I'm just wondering what your intentions are toward my sister, Leo."

"You ate fucking grumpy flakes for breakfast this morning, didn't you?"

"Didn't seem to bother you until I changed the topic."

"Charlotte and I are happy just the way things are."

Logan stopped punching and turned to Cowboy. "You're not going to marry her?"

"Not that it's any of your business, but she doesn't want to get married."

"Bullshit. She married Rick."

"Exactly. She married Rick, and look how that turned out."

"Son of a bitch. You can't convince her?"

"I meant what I said. We're happy together."

"You don't know her like I do. She's broken inside. That loser made her think she was worthless."

Cowboy nodded. "I know that, too. But I treat her like the most important person in the world, because that's just what she is to me. Nothing would make me happier than making her my wife, but the idea doesn't make her happy at all. Not much I can do about that."

Logan cursed under his breath and took off his boxing gloves. "I'm sorry, man. I just assumed you were dragging your feet."

"And you wanted to beat somebody up. I get it. But maybe you should go talk to Gemma instead of throwing rocks at everybody else's windows."

27

"Bette Davis."
Who is Bette Davis?
I'll take The Silver Screen for two hundred, Alex.
"Bing Crosby."
Who is Bing Crosby?
Gemma rolled her eyes. Her father couldn't remember his own name or hers, but he could sweep this whole category.
It was one of his better days.
"Dad?"
"James Stewart."
Who is Jimmy Stewart?
She cleared her throat. "Mr. Faraday?"
"Yeah?"
Definitely one of his better days.
"You're going to be a grandfather."
His eyes filled with wonder. "I am?"
"Yes."
"Bev?" he called out. "Beverly, come in here. You're not going to believe this."

Her heart broke a little more than she ever knew it could. "Mama's not here, Daddy."

"Well, where'd she go?"

She hesitated. "The store. She'll be back soon."

"Does she know about the baby?"

"She does. And she's very happy."

"I'll bet she is." He patted her knee. "A grandbaby. I'd never thought I'd see the day, since you had cancer."

Her mouth dropped open, time standing still. "What did you say?"

"The doctors said you wouldn't have any babies, and here you are. That's just wonderful, sweetie. I couldn't be happier for you."

She looked into his watery eyes. "Dad?"

"Yeah?"

Gemma threw her arms around her father. "I love you." She held onto him tightly.

"I love you, too."

She was crying now, so happy to have him back in this moment.

"Gene Kelly," said her father.

She squeezed her eyes shut.

Who is Orson Wells?

No, sorry.

Who is Gene Kelly?

That's right.

I'll take Hollywood Misfits for one hundred.

Her arms dropped. "Dad?"

"Orson Wells."

She sat down in a chair with a thud. Her father had shown her a glimpse, a momentary visit from the man she knew and loved, and for that she was grateful.

She wished she could tell him about Logan, but she

could tell her father was already gone back into his shell. She pulled out her cell phone and sent Logan a text.

COME FOR DINNER.

WE NEED TO TALK.

It was high time she face the father of her child and share her news with someone who would care as much as she did. Hopefully he'd be happy, but she was prepared if he was not.

She said goodbye to her father and walked through the grocery store in a distracted haze. What did she want Logan's reaction to be? She didn't know for the life of her if this day would end discussing custody agreements or with him sharing her bed.

God, she hoped for the latter.

You were the one who broke it off with him.

If you want Logan in your bed, you're going to have to apologize.

She showered and washed her hair, choosing to keep it loose and curling around her shoulders, then picked a soft, too-big tunic wide a wide neck, imagining Logan would like the feel of the fabric before he lifted it over her head.

I am a horny monster.

Maybe it was the baby making her feel like this, or maybe it had just been too long since she'd touched him. But gone were her buzzing concerns about his age, and in their place was warm desire that refused to be contained.

She measured out seasonings and sautéd onions for the risotto. She hadn't made a real home-cooked meal in ages, and it gave her something to do besides worry over Logan's reaction to her pregnancy or imagine him making love to her. The chicken was roasting in the oven and she was stirring the risotto as it simmered on the stove.

He's going to be in shock.

Try not to get too upset by his reaction.

Thirty-year-old guys weren't expecting their girlfriends—or whatever the hell she was to him—to announce they were pregnant. Especially since they'd used protection every time.

Really old, really bad protection.

He'd better not ask her if it was his. She might have to smack him in the face if he did that.

In the two weeks she'd been home from the hospital, she'd had lots of time to consider what kind of mother she would be after spending years focusing only on her career.

When she found out she couldn't have kids she'd spent so much time villainizing motherhood in her own mind, her own version of sour grapes. Now she was trading in a high-powered job for homemade baby food and dirty diapers.

Hell, my job is already gone.

She stopped stirring the rice, suddenly remembering how she had once longed to be a family court judge, helping kids find good homes. She'd done an about-face when she found out she couldn't have kids of her own, not wanting to see so many of their sweet faces. She could go back to that now. Do what she'd always wanted to do.

She probably wouldn't get to be a judge again, but she could still work in the system. Advocate for those kids without a voice.

The doorbell rang and she took a shaking breath in. This was it.

Logan.

God, she'd missed him. She considered launching herself into his arms and swallowing him up.

Relax.

Take it easy.

She moved the risotto off the heat and wiped her hands

on her apron. He'd given her the time she needed to think, but she'd also realized just how much she longed to have him next to her when he wasn't around.

And while she certainly missed the sex, it wasn't what she missed most. She simply missed *him*.

She walked to the front door.

He was smart—at least as smart as she was—and funny, and insightful, and sweet...

She pulled it open with a smile on her face, anticipation turning to shock in an instant when she realized her visitor wasn't Logan at all.

"What are you doing here?"

Anthony Royce took two steps into her brownstone and knocked her out with one punch.

28

Cowboy's headlights lit up the dirt road as he made his way to the outdoor shooting range just outside downtown Atlanta. He'd been home in bed with Charlotte when Jessa called, concerned because she didn't know where Jax was and he wasn't answering his phone.

It was June eleventh, which meant Cowboy immediately knew where to look.

Seven years ago to the day, Jax had started HERO Force with a staff of three: Hawk, Garrison Cole and Cowboy. The night of HERO Force's first anniversary, Jax and Cowboy shot Cole, dead.

A pothole rocked his old Blazer. It had been dark that night, too—a moonless night that made it difficult to see, though in his memory everything about that night had been hard to interpret.

Back then, Jax had been pretty active in local politics, convinced he needed the approval of the officials to have HERO Force be a success. But that particular night, he hadn't felt like going to Royce's campaign fundraiser and had sent Garrison in his place.

Garrison, with his PTSD and drinking problem.

Royce showed up the next day in a rage, saying Garrison had molested his twelve year-old daughter the night before. Cowboy told him to call the police, but Royce refused. "Do you know what they'll do to her at the police station, and worse, at the trial? Where is Garrison? I'll handle it myself."

Cowboy had driven his brand new Blazer to the shooting range with Royce and Jax in tow, right down this same road. Garrison was there trying out some new weapons, or so he'd said.

But when they arrived, Cowboy shined his headlights across the open field, and there—sitting in the grass in the middle of the range—was Garrison.

"Took you long enough," he'd said.

Royce was irate. He walked into the field. "I know what you did to my daughter, you son of a bitch."

That's when Cowboy saw Royce held up a pistol. "Put down the gun, Anthony."

"Doesn't matter to me," said Garrison. The steel of the semi-automatic in his hands gleamed in the headlights. "I've been sitting here all day thinking about eating one of these bullets."

Royce shouted. "I'll shoot you!"

Suddenly, a deer darted in front of Cowboy's SUV and he slammed on the brakes, adrenaline rushing into his bloodstream and focusing his attention back on the present. Sure enough, Jax's truck was pulled off to the side of the road.

Cowboy pulled in behind it, honking his horn twice to alert Jax to his presence. He left his headlights on, just as he had that fateful night six years ago.

"You didn't need to come out here," said Jax.

"Jessa's looking for you." Cowboy sat down next to him. "You never told her about Garrison?"

Jax took a drag of a cigarette, the orange tip glowing brightly. "You ever tell Charlotte?"

"Nope." Cowboy hadn't seen him smoke in years, the smell of it bringing him back in time to the night Garrison was killed.

Cowboy could see Garrison in the headlights, Royce threatening to kill him. He and Jax had come up on either side of Royce, prepared to stop him from firing.

"It's a hard thing, killing yourself," said Garrison. "I should know. I've tried it several times." He cocked his head. "Maybe I've been doing it all wrong." Just like that, he trained his weapon on Royce.

Cowboy pulled his gun and fired at Garrison. Jax did, too.

Garrison fell to the ground, gasping for breath.

"I didn't mean to do it," he cried.

Cowboy ran to him, falling to the ground by his side. "Call 9-1-1."

"I thought she was older. I was drunk."

Royce's voice was cold. "I hope you burn in hell." One last shot rang out, this one hitting Garrison in the head.

Jax took a drag of his cigarette. "I swear, I still hear the shots out here at night."

"He had his demons."

"Suicide by SEAL," said Jax. "He wanted us to kill him so he wouldn't have to do it himself."

"We didn't have a choice."

"Nope."

"Give me one of those." Cowboy's cell phone rang. "That's probably your wife."

"Tell her I'm not here."

"You've got it." Cowboy pulled it out. "It's Logan." He answered it. "What's up?"

"Gemma's missing and so is her security guard. I need backup. We have to find her."

29

Gemma's shoulders ached from having her hands tied for so long behind the dining chair back, but she didn't dare complain.

Royce moved to the opposite side of the table and sat down. "I never should have slept with you," he said, eyes full of disdain.

"It was a long time ago."

He blew out air. "Not long enough, because here you are, fucking up my life all over again."

She tilted her head. "What did I do?"

"You told HERO Force where to find me. That must have been you."

"And you shot me and left me for dead," she said.

"I ran out of bullets. You got lucky."

"Lucky." She shook her head at his choice of words. "How did I get the concussion?"

He grinned. "The van window was down. I slammed your head against the door frame. I couldn't have you screaming and letting the others know I was there."

"There's only one thing I don't understand. I've spent a

lot of time thinking about the ransom Cole wanted for you—a guilty verdict against Jax and Cowboy in my court. But how did they know the men wouldn't opt for a jury trial?"

He clucked his tongue. "I'm disappointed in you, Gemma. I thought you were smarter than this. Cole had no idea whether the men of HERO Force would opt for a jury trial or not."

Her mouth opened. "But you did."

"They'd already filed their pleas by the time I was…taken."

"You staged your own kidnapping."

"Not entirely. Cole was there, along with some of his friends from the county jail. I just told them what to do."

"And the bomb that killed Barbara?"

"That was just a bonus." He stood and walked to a sideboard, pouring himself a drink. "That woman had been bleeding the life out of me for years. It was well past her time to move on."

He'd treated her badly in life, then he precipitated her death. "You could have just divorced her."

He shook his head. "No. That wouldn't have worked out nearly as well for me. My parents were peach growers. Her parents were in microprocessors. This is their house, actually." He held out his arms to encompass the extravagance around them.

Gemma's stare bounced from the golden chandelier to the high ceilings and two-foot crown moldings. "It's just a house, Royce."

"That's where you're wrong. It's my house, and so are the apartment downtown and the ranch outside of Buckhead. There's even a cute little place in Switzerland." He put his hand on his chest, fingers splayed. "While I'm sure life without my beloved Barbara will be difficult to take, these small creature comforts will surely provide me with some pleasure."

Eight years had changed Royce from someone she admired and respected to a foul-spirited villain. She couldn't believe she'd ever found him attractive.

"Why are you staring at me like that?" he asked.

"You're different than you used to be."

"You mean when we were together?"

She nodded.

He stood and walked slowly toward her. The back of her neck burned and she refused to lift her head. He bent down so that his eyes were even with hers. "I'm not so different than I used to be."

He reached out and twirled a piece of her hair around his finger. "I could show you, if you'd like."

She jerked her head to the side, pulling the hair out of his grasp.

"That's right," he said. "You've moved on to that little boy. What's his name? Logan."

Her stomach seemed to fall through the floor. "Leave him out of this."

"Oh, I'm sorry, but I can't do that. You're the one who put him between us. Now he's been making waves down at the courthouse, searching for government plates that very closely match my own."

"You! Why would you try to hurt me? Come to my house with a gun?"

"I said it was my car, sweetie. Not my gun and certainly not myself at the scene. Though I admit I was looking forward to a clean break from the women in my life. *Such leeches.*"

"That's it? Just because we used to go out, you wanted me dead? Have you lost your mind?"

"You were the one who made it unpleasant whenever our paths would cross, Gemma."

She gaped. "Because you lied to me, pretending you weren't married so that I looked like the office tramp, and my entire career was nearly ruined by gossip and conjecture!"

"Still. I didn't enjoy seeing you out and about." He checked his watch.

"Am I keeping you from something?"

"I'm surprised they're not here yet."

"Who?"

"HERO Force, of course. I'm assuming your little knight in shining braces is going come looking for you, but then again, maybe not. I have more faith in Jax and Leo, however. I left the address on your kitchen counter like a big, red flag. They should be here soon."

Her mouth was dry. "What happens when they get here?"

"Did you see the car bomb that killed my wife?"

She nodded.

"That was like the fireworks. This one's going to be the finale."

30

Logan sat in the passenger seat of his Ferrari, Cowboy at the wheel. A computer was open on Logan's lap. "The house was owned by Royce's wife. She inherited it when her parents passed away."

"So Royce is leading us to his lair, basically," said Cowboy.

Logan nodded. "Right."

"Awesome." Cowboy barely slowed down for a sharp turn.

"Jesus Cowboy, watch it."

"If I had this car, I wouldn't need to date your sister. I could have an orgasm just...driving."

"Thanks so much for that visual. I still think we should call the police."

"You might be right, but if we do, they're not going to let us anywhere near that building. Are you ready to hand Gemma's safety over to the men in blue?"

"Not with Royce. He's already killed his wife. The man doesn't have anything to lose."

"I'm thinking that was the point. Lose her. Take all her money. Now he's got everything he wanted."

"Except he didn't expect us to get in his way."

Cowboy nodded. "Exactly." The tires squealed as he hugged another turn.

"I don't know what's worse, letting you drive this thing or having Hawk pilot the bird."

"Hawk pilot the bird. Touch base with them. See where they are."

Logan pulled out his cell phone and called Jax. "They just landed on the other side of the property. Why'd you want them so far away?"

"I think Royce might have a special welcome set up for us at the main entrance. I don't want him taking out the whole team."

"I get it. So he'll just take out us."

"Relax, Logan. I'm not as dumb as I look, okay? He's got a penchant for explosives, but that's my thing. I know what I'm looking for."

"Just remember, Gemma's in there somewhere."

"I didn't forget."

"And she's carrying my child."

Cowboy turned his head to look at Logan. "No shit?"

Logan pointed out the windshield. "Watch the damn road."

"Congratulations, man. I mean you're happy about it, right?"

"I'm a little freaked out, to be honest, but yeah. I like her a lot."

"Always a good thing for the parents of an impending person to like each other."

"I didn't say she liked me."

Cowboy pointed to an exit. "Is that my turn?"

"Yeah. Slow down." The Ferrari slid down the off-ramp like a child's toy on a track. "Cut the lights," said Logan. "It's just ahead."

A wide mansion came into view in the distance, it's silhouette reminding Logan of the White House.

"How are we going to find her in there?" asked Logan.

"Easy. Royce wants her to be found. The trick is to get in and get the girl without getting ourselves blown up."

Cowboy parked the car in the woods surrounding the property. The men grabbed their packs, weapons and earpieces. "We're going in," said Cowboy.

"Affirmative. We're heading in from the back of the property," said Hawk.

Logan was holding binoculars to his eyes. His heart leaped into his chest. "I see her. Right there, in the big window to the right of the front door. She's tied to a dining room chair. No sign of Royce."

"That's what I call bait. I've got ten bucks says we're in for a bait 'n' switch by the time we get up there. Come on."

When the reached the end of the canopied forest, they stopped to regroup. "See that fire escape up the back side of the house?" Cowboy asked. "We go there. Climb up and get access to the roof, so we can get back down through a stairwell, duct, or courtyard."

"That's what he's expecting us to do," said Logan. "I say we march right up to the front door and let ourselves in."

"Too dangerous. It's completely lit up. We'll be sitting ducks for this guy."

"He would have covered the roof, Cowboy. It's the most obvious point of entry."

Cowboy sighed. "You want to go in the front fucking door."

"Yes."

"We need cover."

Logan looked from the woods to the house. "That's about twelve hundred yards."

Cowboy talked into his microphone. "Hawk can you make a kill shot from twelve hundred yards?"

"I'm not a sniper, Cowboy."

"I can do it," said Logan.

Cowboy met his stare.

Hawk's voice came over their earpieces. "Logan's a better shot than I am."

Cowboy narrowed his eyes. "Twelve hundred yards."

"Wind out of the northwest, eight miles an hour. I can make it, Leo." He held out his hand for the high powered rifle. "I've got your six."

Cowboy put the gun in Logan's hand and nodded his head once. "Going in the front door."

"Right."

Logan turned around, quickly spotting a tree he could climb for some height. By the time he got up there and turned around, Leo was gone. He pulled out his binoculars and night vision goggles, easily spotting the HERO Force men. He got into position, scanning the windows for any sign of Royce.

31

Royce left the room nearly an hour ago, leaving Gemma in front of the window like a mannequin on display.

Don't fall for it, Logan.

She didn't know where Royce had gone, but she knew he was using her to lure the HERO Force team to her rescue, and he would do everything in his power to ensure none of them survived.

She bit her lip. Her left arm was completely numb from her shoulder down to her thumb. Her right she could still feel, the nerve endings screaming with pain.

A dog growled from the hallway and her head whipped around. It was a large breed, dark brown, and it was baring it's teeth. She was terrified of any dog bigger than a Cocker Spaniel, and that was when her hands were free to defend herself.

"Nice doggie," she whispered. "Good boy."

The dog barked ferociously, his jaws chomping, and she squealed with fright.

Royce called in the distance, "Just ignore Fluffy. He's here to greet our guests."

"Are they here?"

"The helicopter arrived forty minutes ago. I'm surprised they haven't made their grand entrance yet. Surely they can see the merchandise I have to offer."

The growling dog got closer and barked again. "Please Royce, get it away from me!"

He didn't answer.

The slightest noise came from the window and she turned back the other way. There it was again, pelting the glass like hail or loud rain. A small light flashed outside, like someone waking their cell phone.

They're here.

Her breathing sped up, so afraid was she for the men outside.

Please don't let me hyperventilate again.

The dog suddenly darted for the window and began to bark consistently. Fear made her want to throw up, but she called the dog to her side as cheerfully as she could muster. "Come here, boy. Come on! What's your name? Are you hungry?"

"Leave him alone!" Royce yelled.

She stared into the black window, pantomiming that she could hear him yelling. The dog growled at her some more and got right up next to her leg, drool hanging from his chops.

"Good boy," she whispered, certain he would latch those sharp teeth onto her skin at any moment. But Logan was outside somewhere, and she had to keep Royce from finding out.

The doorbell rang.

The dog went nuts, barking and running toward it.

Royce appeared in the hallway with what looked like a small machine gun. "They never cease to amaze, do they?"

He seemed to be considering what to do next. The doorbell rang again, making the dog bark with renewed fervor.

"Get the door," said Royce.

"Me? I can't move."

"I'll untie you." He looked at the tall windows, then turned off the lights and crossed to her. The bell continued to ring as he worked to unfasten her wrists. "Undo your ankles."

"I can't feel my arms."

"You're not trying to be helpful!"

"I'm sorry..."

He bent down in front of her chair to undo them himself. With the room dark, she could see outside the window to the lawn and the trees beyond it.

HERO Force wouldn't send all its men to the front door. Someone was hanging back, covering the others. She closed her eyes and prayed. If he had night vision goggles, he might be able to see into the house.

The moment her ankles were free, she threw herself on the floor. The dog ran to her, biting at her clothes and skin, and she screamed.

"Get up!" yelled Royce. He moved to her, trying to pull her to a stand, but she evaded him. He stood. "You're making this difficult. Get up and the dog will leave you alone."

A small sound rang out like the glass falling on Logan's countertop.

Royce fell to the ground, but she couldn't see him. "Royce?" she called. The dog was quiet now, licking something. And then she smelled the metallic scent of blood.

Forcing her tingling legs to bear weight, she hobbled to the light switch and turned it on. Royce was facedown on the carpet, a dark pool spreading around him, the dog licking it up.

She spun around and yelled as loudly as she could. "Royce is dead! I'm opening the door. It's Gemma!" She unlocked it and the men swarmed in.

"Good work, Doc," said Cowboy into his mic. "You got him." His eyes went to Gemma's. "She's fine. Come on down."

32

Gemma walked along the wooden dock, hugging herself against the chill in the air, a satisfied smile on her face. It was the end of a perfect summer day, a cool breeze coming off the lake and the sun setting in the sky with a showy display of orange and pink.

Logan had brought her here, saying the place belonged to a friend. He grilled her a meal on the wide porch of the log cabin and amused her with stories of his life, from his childhood in rural Pennsylvania to his most recent promotion of sorts with HERO Force.

Now she was full, and it struck her the feeling was as much in her spirit as it was in her stomach. Since learning of her pregnancy she'd opened her heart to the possibility of a relationship with Logan. Surely they would have a relationship of some kind, if only for the child.

And if she wanted more than that, well maybe that would be okay, too. She sighed. She needed to tell him about the baby, but she didn't want to upset their tenuous harmony.

Footsteps shook the dock beneath her feet and she

turned to see him coming toward her.

Damn, he's hot.

Any woman in the world would feel a little faint if he were advancing on her, and she let herself really feel it in the pit of her stomach like a childhood crush.

He reached her, his stare intense. "You make quite a picture out here, with your blue dress and the lake and the sunset behind you."

"Thank you."

"I had a nice day."

It had been nice. Maybe the nicest day she could remember. Such a stupid, sappy little word that meant you almost loved it. Or, at least, she had. "Me, too."

"But there's something we need to talk about," he said.

"Uh oh."

He met her eyes. "I know about the baby."

The dock beneath her feet seemed to sink deeper into the lake and her face heated. "How?"

"A nurse in the hospital let it slip. I kept waiting for you to say something. Why didn't you tell me?"

She felt dizzy. Angry. "She had no right to do that."

"No, but I'm glad someone did."

She turned away from him. This conversation was happening too quickly and completely out of her control. "You've known this whole time."

"Yes, and I'm happy, Gemma. Are you?"

Was he out of his mind?

"Of course I'm happy. I thought I couldn't have children and now I'm having a baby."

"With me."

"Yes, with you."

He lifted his chin. "Are you happy about that part?"

She turned back. "I know it's not fair to you. I'm sorry."

"Hey." He put his hands on her upper arms. "I'm not asking if it's fair, and please don't apologize for the greatest thing in my life to-date. I'm asking if you're happy I'm the father of your child."

"The greatest thing in your life to-date?"

He shrugged. "I'm excited. Aren't you?"

"Well yes, but I didn't think you would be."

He ran a hand through his hair. "Why not? I love kids, and I couldn't pick a better mom."

"Than me?" She laughed. "I have no idea how to do this. I'll probably diaper the poor thing's head."

"You're strong and smart. You'll teach our child to be strong and smart, too." He touched her cheek. "And she'll be beautiful."

He was leaning into her, going in for a kiss, and suddenly Gemma didn't know what any of it meant. Logan was talking about nice days and fatherhood and a teensy bit about forever and she was confused, like she'd be agreeing to something by kissing him—something she didn't even understand.

Logan stared at her for a long moment, the sound of water lapping at the dock the only sound in her ears.

"Do you like me?" he asked. "Or am I just the guy you got stuck with?"

"Definitely not stuck. I like you a lot." She licked her lips. "Since I found out I was pregnant I've been trying to change my thinking. To let you in. Just be patient with me while we figure out the details."

"I can do that."

He kissed her softly, tenderly, and for the first time she admitted to herself how much she cared for him. Leaning back in his arms, she took in his strong features and the soul-searing look in his eyes.

33

Seven months later

Logan O'Malley was chasing an invisible man.

"C'mon, you motherfucker. Come out where I can see you." He leaned forward, his face only inches from his screen, fingers punching out commands in a staccato rhythm that was second nature to his brain.

Hundreds of lines of code scrolled down the screen, his eyes scanning the familiar words and variable strings like an interpreter scanning a document in a foreign language. His stomach growled but he ignored it, his foot tapping incessantly on the floor.

He'd been sitting here for hours, following the labyrinth back to it's beginning, stalking the one person who didn't want to be found.

Austin rolled his chair over next to Logan's, peering over his shoulder. "I got me one of them Minecraft accounts. You play Minecraft?"

Logan shushed him. "I've almost got this son of a bitch." His mind was unravelling the invisible man's method of attack, following the clues that led back to the all-important lines of code capable of undermining an entire company.

The directory. It must be hidden in the file structure itself.

He delved deeper.

"My niece wants me to build shit with her," said Austin. "Bunkers and battlefields and tanks and crap. When did girls stop playing with Barbie dolls?"

Noah piped up from across the room, where he sat cleaning his gun. "They still play with Barbie dolls, but they kick some ass before they put on their little plastic shoes and let Ken take them out for dinner."

Austin cocked his head. "I'll bet you Ken never got laid. He looks like the kind of dude chicks string along for years before giving it away to some musician in a closet backstage."

"Or a Navy SEAL," said Noah.

The men laughed.

"Shut up," said Logan, narrowing his eyes. It was here somewhere. Everything pointed to this directory. He typed a series of commands, his whole screen filling up with code.

"The limiting strand is pointing to a wildcard value," he said.

Yes!

There it was. The needle in the haystack, the one line of code that didn't belong. Logan let out a loud whoop. "Gotcha, you stupid son of a bitch."

He opened a new screen and began typing, his fingers flying across the keys. One small program to set his trap. Another line of code to close it on the invisible man, shut it down, lock him out forever.

Or at least until he came back to life as someone else, found another way in. But that was a problem for another day. "Take that, you motherfucker." He hit enter and flew backwards on his wheeled chair, watching the next sequence unfold in real time.

USER DELETED appeared on row after row, the screen scrolling until it was filled with them. He raised both arms and hollered in victory. Austin and Noah clapped lamely behind him.

Jax entered the room and leaned on Logan's desk, crossing his arms over his chest. "All done playing Dungeons and Dragons?"

Logan pointed to the screen. "That was not a game. That was me putting the nails in the coffin of the Yakimoto assignment. Not only did I find their hacker, I traced him back to his server and dismantled his entire line of attack."

Logan rolled over to a sleek printer and pulled off a sheet of paper. "Gary Fitzsimmons. A computer programmer for AuCen Corp, Yakimoto's biggest competitor."

Jax took the paper and shook his head. "Nice work, Doc. We didn't expect to nail this guy so quickly."

"I think you ought to buy me lunch."

"I'll do one better. I've got a bottle of whiskey in the conference room."

"Can we come too, boss?" asked Austin. "Me and Noah here were instrumental in the computer hacking thing-a-ma-bobber."

"Yeah," said Noah. "I held his mouse pad."

Jax shook his head. "Come on, you boneheads. Relax for a few. We're going wheels up the day after tomorrow. Got a cult in the mountains of Idaho we've got to infiltrate."

"Idaho's got mountains?" asked Noah, making Austin snort.

Logan walked around the bend, the glass wall of the conference room coming into view, all the members of

HERO Force standing around a cake, the room decorated with pink and blue balloons.

"Ashley thought we should throw you a baby shower," said Jax. "We figured since it's the only thing she's done for us is reproduce, she should have the honors."

A big, goofy grin took over Logan's face. "You shouldn't have, guys."

A bleached blonde with long curly hair opened her arms wide. "Congratulations! I'm Ashley. I'm so happy for you."

"Thanks." He furrowed his brow. "Do you work here?"

She bobbed her head. "I went out on maternity leave a few days after Jax hired me. Bedrest. You guys were all in Kabul or something."

"Okay. Well, thanks for the party."

"You're just going to love being a parent," she said.

Logan sat down in front of a cake decorated with tiny combat boots, one pink and one blue. The background was pink and blue camouflage. "This is awesome."

Charlotte threw her arms around Cowboy's neck and settled herself on his lap. "Two more weeks, brother boy, and I get to be an aunt."

"And I'm going to be a father."

"How's Gemma doing?"

"Good. Great."

Crappy.

"She's just glowing."

Like a scary Jack-o-lantern who hates me.

"You're going to make a great dad." Charlotte leaned forward and hugged him, squishing Logan's head right next to Cowboy's.

"Oh, you made it!" Charlotte exclaimed.

Logan turned around to see Gemma standing in the

doorway. He crossed to her and hugged her, her belly pressing into his.

"I'm so glad you're here!" said Ashley.

Gemma leaned into Logan's chest, whispering in his ear, "Who is that?"

"Apparently she works here. Her name is Ashley."

"So nice to meet you," said Ashley, throwing her arms around Gemma.

"Oh, please. Please, get off me."

Jax walked over and hugged Gemma. "You're looking good, kid."

Gemma burst out crying.

Logan's eyes went wide. Jax patted him on the shoulder. "Any day now, Doc."

"I'm sorry," Gemma wailed. "I didn't want to ruin your party. But I wasn't feeling well and the doctor had me come in, and my blood pressure's a little high and they're going to induce me..."

"When?" asked Charlotte.

"Now. Right now." She gestured down the hall with her thumb. "They made me come in a wheelchair."

"Oh my God!" Logan panicked. "Stay here. I'll get the wheelchair and we'll go."

"It's just next door, Logan. They let me borrow an orderly."

"No, I'm going to push you. I'm going to push. That's the least I can do. Are we ready? Should we go? Are we ready?"

Gemma started to cry again.

He grabbed her shoulders. "What's the matter, honey?"

She sniveled. "I really wanted some cake."

34

Gemma got up from the rocker and put baby Ian into his crib. He was sound asleep, his mouth open in a perfect cupid's bow.

She tiptoed from the room, closing the door quietly behind her and walking through the apartment to Logan's chair in his solitary circle of light.

He looked up when she got there. "Is he sleeping?"

She nodded.

"I thought you said you were tired."

"I am." She took a deep breath. "But I want you to sleep with me."

"Are you sure? I mean, can we...is it time?"

She nodded. She walked to the bed with him right behind her, more nervous than a virgin on her wedding night. She pulled back the covers and slipped inside. He crawled in beside her, opening his arms for her to curl against his side.

She rested her head on his chest and his arm came around her back, gently stroking. Her knee slipped between his legs, as naturally as if it belonged there.

He felt so good in her arms after so much time, and the natural distance that came with new parenthood. Her hand explored his muscled chest, then up to his shoulder, her nails lightly scraping their way down his arm. He moaned deep in his throat and grabbed her wrist.

"You don't have to do this," he said. "We can just cuddle if you want."

She lifted her face to his. "I want to." She looked at his lips. "I never stopped wanting to." They kissed, his arm tightening around her back, and she moved on top of him. She took control of their kiss, gently tasting him and sucking on his bottom lip. She could feel his growing erection beneath her, and her hips moved against him suggestively.

In the six weeks since they'd become a family, every one of her defenses had fallen away. Where she once thought Logan was too young, he was now simply her baby's father, and she knew Ian was lucky to have such a wonderful role model.

His mouth moved to the column of her neck, lightly sucking, teasing her skin, and her breath caught in her throat. She sat up, sliding her hands underneath his shirt and pushing the fabric up until he pulled it over his head.

She lifted her own shirt and threw it to the floor. His hands came up and squeezed her breasts before unhooking her bra and pulling it down her arms.

"You're so fucking beautiful," he said, sitting up to kiss her.

She pushed him back down. "I love you, Logan."

He held her face in his hands. "I love you, too."

"I'm sorry it took me so long to say. I was so emotional with the baby, and so scared we were together for the wrong reasons. But now, I look at you a hundred times in a day and that's the only thing that goes through my mind. I love you."

"I've loved you since the first night you spent with me."

"I know." She knelt between his legs and freed him from his briefs, taking him into her mouth and making him gasp.

She climbed up his body and straddled him, holding him at her entrance and slowly sinking down on top of him.

He rolled her over and held himself above her. "Is it okay?"

"Yes."

He thrust into her deeply, piercing the armor she'd used to surround herself from his love.

After they'd exhausted themselves, the shadows of the loft came back into view, their labored breathing perfectly in synch. She kissed his damp temple. "I'm glad you're here with me," she whispered.

He kissed her collarbone, slowly moving over to the curve of her shoulder. "And I always will be."

AUSTIN IS SEPARATED FROM HERO FORCE ON A MISSION TO RECOVER A YOUNG WOMAN FROM A DANGEROUS CULT.

Buy Targeted by the SEAL

Sign up for Amy Gamet's mailing list
or text BOOKS to 66866

A portion of the proceeds from *Justice for the SEAL* will be donated to the Triple Negative Breast Cancer Foundation.

A note from the author

PLEASE TAKE a moment to leave a review. Writing is solitary work, and feedback from readers puts a smile on my face and helps to counteract things like my kids calling me "the fun ender" and having to do laundry. (I really hate laundry.)

If you're reading on a kindle, note that the "rate this

book" feature at the end of an book is not the same as leaving a review. Only Amazon sees those ratings and the stars have no effect on the star rating of the book.

The number of reviews and their star-rating determine where I can advertise and promote my books. They also help other readers make purchasing decisions.

This link will take you back to write a review at the retailer where you bought this book. Thank you so much for taking the time!

All the best,

Amy Gamet

Made in the USA
Monee, IL
07 August 2024